The
Pets

The
Pets

Bragi Ólafsson

Translated from the Icelandic
by Janice Balfour

A Novel

OPEN LETTER
LITERARY TRANSLATIONS FROM THE UNIVERSITY OF ROCHESTER

Title of the original Icelandic edition: Gæludýrin
Published by agreement with Forlagid Publishing, www.forlagid.is

The book Armann Valur quotes from on pgs. 26, 27, and 29 is *The Language Instinct* by Steven Pinker. Published by William Morrow & Co., 1994.

Library of Congress Control Number: 2008926608
ISBN-13: 978-1-934824-01-6 / ISBN-10: 1-934824-01-1

Printed on acid-free paper in the United States of America.

Text set in Goudy, an old style serif originally designed by Frederic W. Goudy (1865–1947).

Design by N. J. Furl

Open Letter is the University of Rochester's nonprofit, literary translation press: Lattimore Hall 411, Box 270082, Rochester, NY 14627

www.openletterbooks.org

Some enchanted evening
You may see a stranger,
You may see a stranger
Across a crowded room;
—Oscar Hammerstein II

Part
One

The Lottery Prize

1

Someone, wearing an anorak, knocked on my door at lunchtime. My neighbor Tomas is out pottering in the garden and hears me when I open the garden gate. He welcomes me home from my trip abroad and tells me that some fellow—he couldn't say how old he was—was hanging around outside my front door around twelve-thirty.

"He was wearing some kind of blue nylon anorak with a hood," he says. "I couldn't see his face properly because of his hood."

Tomas himself is wearing an anorak, and has a knitted cap on his head, as well as a scarf with the colors of some English football team around his neck.

"Maybe he was at the wrong house," I say.

"I don't think so," Tomas answers. "Somehow I got the feeling that he knew where he was going. He had a plastic bag in his hand, that I think he put down in the snow while he waited to see if you were at home. He knocked for a good five or ten minutes."

At this moment I can't think of anyone who needs to talk to me today—Tuesday, at lunchtime, when I'm not even in the country—but when Tomas mentions the plastic bag, for one second I'm afraid that it could have been Sigurvin, an old work mate, and that the bag contained recently purchased warm beer, though it would have probably cooled down a lot in February's frost. This fellow Sigurvin was supposed to have stopped drinking, but the memory of him drunk was so vivid and terrifying that it still bothered me.

"You didn't notice if he took unusually large strides?" I ask.

Tomas says that he hadn't really paid him much attention, just noticed how long he stayed banging at the door. But, come to think of it, he had also seen the man peer through the kitchen window, as if he expected me to be hiding in there. The fact that the fellow peered through the kitchen window when it was obvious that no one was at home made me think of another old acquaintance. However, as far as I know, it's impossible, or at least very unlikely, that he is here in Reykjavik.

"There was something about him that gave me the feeling he was in need of shelter," Tomas says, and I'm not sure if he is joking. "Then I noticed that he was fiddling with the name plate on the door. It looked as if he was polishing it. Probably just wiping the snow off so that he could read the name properly."

These fine copper or brass name plates give a sense of endurance and eternity. Some old atmosphere lingers from bygone days. My name plate is only two years old and yet it is so weather-beaten that one imagines its owner is old or neither old nor young; it's almost like a grave stone. The main difference being that there are no dates or title on it, like "managing director" or "ship owner"—as one sees in cemeteries—and no wish that the owner rest in peace, in this instance inside his own front door.

I ask Tomas if he spoke to the man at all. He says that he had been thinking of telling him that I was abroad, but had decided not to; not that he was hinting that this acquaintance of mine was by any means dubious, but one could never be sure if such men would take advantage of the fact that the flat was empty.

"*Such* men?" I repeat. "What do you mean by *such*?"

"Oh, I just meant, you know, ordinary men."

"So he was only an *ordinary* man?" I say and emphasize the word *ordinary* so it is quite obvious that I am joking.

"I suppose so," Tomas says. "I didn't see anything peculiar about him really, come to think of it."

"By the way, how did *you* know that I was abroad?" I ask with a smile. Tomas smiles back and says that Bella, the old lady who lives in the flat above me, had asked him to keep an eye on the house last weekend while she was away visiting her sister in Akranes because she had promised, he said, to look after my flat while I was in America. Then she had started talking about me, said she couldn't have been luckier with her neighbor, that it made such a difference sharing a house with people one could trust. I correct Tomas: I had only gone to London, Bella must have misunderstood me.

"So you didn't see his face?" I ask, trying to steer the conversation back to the original subject matter and put an end to it. Standing out here in the frost is killing me.

"No, I didn't," he answers, seeming to realize that I want to get indoors. "He was too well hidden inside the hood."

I had told Bella before I left that I would be away for two weeks—though I don't remember telling her where I was going—and she promised (without me asking) to keep an eye on the flat in the meantime. She even offered to water my plants and insisted on giving me some cuttings when I told her that I didn't have any in my flat. I declined her offer politely.

At twelve-thirty I was probably moving slowly down the escalator in the direction of the duty-free store or going through the customs with my suitcases and bags. At the very moment when this fellow in the anorak decided that he had knocked long enough—was maybe even trying to peer through the kitchen window—I was probably getting on the bus outside the airport. Perhaps I had sat down beside Greta, the woman I got to know on the plane just before we landed and on the bus to Reykjavik. I realize that I am forgetting her features little by little. I can't form a clear image of her, despite the fact that I first met her fifteen years ago, saw her occasionally after that, and saw her again today on the flight. It's strange how quickly faces fade in one's memory. The only things I can remember clearly are her wavy, fair hair, her full lips, and her thin arms—they poked out of the wide sleeves of her T-shirt like two drain pipes. I'll recall small details and particular facial expressions of hers better this evening when we meet. That is, if she calls.

She said she would call. And I'm feeling really guilty because I hope she will. I know Vigdis—my girlfriend or lover (depending on how you look at it)—will call this evening; she said she would give me a ring when I got home.

Before I go in with my bags, Tomas repeats something about being sure that the fellow in the anorak will come back. I tell him that I have an idea of who he is, though in reality I haven't a clue. I have discounted the two men I thought of first and there is no way that it could have been Saebjorn or Jaime. They weren't going to come round until later tonight. Besides, Tomas's description doesn't fit either of them at all.

There is something about my neighbor's face that reminds me of my fellow passenger on the plane, the linguist Armann Valur. Probably the lower half of his face; his mouth and in particular his nose. It's as if Tomas's nose has no definite shape or form, almost as if it's some tiny, useless blob. The grammarian's nose was similar: bent, though it wasn't broken, and the tip of it looked as if it had been melted or squashed under something, I don't dare to imagine what.

When I've said goodbye to Tomas and gone indoors, it suddenly strikes me that it was strange he should be out in the garden at lunchtime, when the man in the anorak knocked at my door, and now again around five when I come home. It's February and everything is covered in snow; what's a man in his sixties doing out in the garden in such weather, twice on the same day? And yet sometimes it's as if people and objects are put in a certain place on earth just to suit the whims of some eccentric; as if someone up above is amusing himself by arranging us as he likes, contrary to all common sense. I have sometimes felt as if I've been picked up by the scruff of my neck and moved, in different situations, either to rescue me from some calamity or—which I suspect is more often the case—to deliberately get me into trouble.

The air in the flat is stale, which is not surprising as the windows haven't been opened for two weeks. I push the bedroom window wide open, but I only open the kitchen window a crack. When the cold, fresh air spreads through the flat I feel it's good to be back home. I tell myself that this is my place. I have been put here, whether it was organized according to a whim of the fellow up above or resulted from a mixture of my own decisions and the unavoidable incidents which, nearly every day, give life just as much color as, for instance, music, sex, films, and books do. This is my home: my everyday world. Then, all at once, I get the feeling that my thoughts are complete nonsense. A peculiar sensation tells me that I should not take for granted the fact that I live here, that this flat is my home rather than someone else's, even though I have lived here alone for nearly two years and haven't made any plans to move in the near future. After a while I manage to shake off this uncanny feeling. This is my home. And I am just about to put "Lonely Fire" from Big Fun on the turntable.

2

When he kicked open the gate it sounded as if it was going to break. When he got out in the street he stopped and looked in both directions. It was very cold; he pulled the hood further down over his head. He spun around when he heard the man in the garden next door, a middle-aged man with a knitted cap on his head, kicking the snow off his boots before going into his house. Then he walked west along Grettisgata, towards the center of town. Four cars came down Frakkastigur, one after another, and turned into Grettisgata. The last one skidded when it rounded the corner and managed to stop just before the rear of it crashed into the wall of a house. He began to walk faster but had to watch his step because the soles of his shoes were so slippery; they were his best shoes, with narrow pointed toes which poked out from under the threadbare bottoms of his long jeans.

At the corner of Klapparstigur and Grettisgata he saw a group of school children standing in front of an antique shop window on the other side of the street. He stopped at the corner for a few seconds, gazed at the children, and banged the heels of his shoes together to get rid of the snow that had collected on them. Then he set off down Klapparstigur, and, after a few steps, he slipped on the icy pavement and nearly landed on his back. He paused, looked around, and then carried on. The traffic on the main street, Laugavegur, seemed to be moving very slowly. Three young girls stood on the corner waiting to cross the road. He, on the other hand, just squeezed out between two cars, slid over the icy road, and mounted the pavement on the other side of Klapparstigur. Then he disappeared into a little bar.

From the outside no one would have guessed that there was any trade going on in there; it looked more like a fisherman's hut or a dilapidated country cottage. Even the name on the sign outside had worn off, if there had been any name there at all.

There was no one inside apart from one member of the staff—a girl of about twenty who was standing in front of a blackboard that was fixed on the wall to the left of the bar. She was writing the day's menu and seemed to be deciding what would be on it as she went along. He walked over to a table in the corner, beside the window, and let go of a worn plastic bag before he sat down. The girl stopped writing on the blackboard and turned around to see who had come in. Then she seemed to get an idea; she started writing again. It was warm inside the bar. The smell of food hung in the air.

3

At the bar in Heathrow I had been musing about the flight home, what we would eat on board and so on. I hoped I wouldn't end up beside a chatterbox or someone who was forever getting up to go to the toilet or talk to other passengers. The last time I flew I sat beside a young man who had tried, without luck, to get me interested in his business (wholesale trade in sportswear and equipment for some peculiar fringe sports) and then rushed back and forth along the aisle, as if that three hour flight was some sort of family or general gathering: Icelanders meeting up after being away from their native soil for at least a week. Really it's no small risk one takes, boarding an airplane. For three hours (not to mention on longer trips) one is locked in a tight, uncomfortable space, way above any civilization, with unpredictable people, who could drink themselves senseless or spill their food and drink over you—and the only place of salvation is the toilet.

I was looking forward to relaxing on board, reading the newspaper I had bought in the airport and perhaps dozing off after the meal. But those plans were to be completely disrupted. I hadn't even sat down in my aisle seat when the man in the middle seat—a rather scruffy fellow of about sixty with a mop of grey hair that was tobacco-colored in patches, who looked like he might smell of alcohol or sweat—made it obvious with his friendly smile that we would enjoy a good chat on the way. While I waited for my turn to put my hand luggage and jacket up in the locker, he offered me an Opal lozenge from a battered box which looked as if it had gotten wet or been sat on. I declined his offer and made an effort to smile and show the appropriate amount of gratitude when he insisted that I take one.

"They are always the same, these air trips," he said when I sat down. I got the feeling that he had been preparing this sentence while I was busy fitting my belongings into the locker. His use of the term *air trips* indicated that he was trying to avoid using the word *flight* in the plural—something that I have always felt was wrong, though I don't know why. When he introduced himself as a linguist a little later—more correctly Armann Valur, linguist and prospective pensioner (this latter title was added more as a joke)—I was rather pleased with myself; I had immediately thought that he had something to do with languages. The power of the subconscious or good intuition, I told myself, smirking at my misfortune in meeting a hulk of a linguist before the pilot had even gotten around to announcing take-off.

I introduced myself to the fellow but got the feeling that he didn't take much notice of my name. I didn't fasten my safety belt straight away, as I half expected him to stand up and take off his dark blue overcoat. He was wearing a suit and a jumper underneath. I took the flight magazine out of the seat pocket and found an article that I could pretend to be engrossed in for a while. It was about the world's most northern golf course, at Akureyri, where Vigdis is staying at the moment. But, just as I feared, I got no peace; the man beside me pointed at the flight attendant who was approaching down the aisle and reminded me to fasten my seatbelt. The "dears" are coming to make sure everyone is strapped in. I expected him to carry on talking, but when he paused I used the opportunity to get my portable tape player out of my bag in the locker. I was back in my seat with my belt fastened before the flight attendant walked past with a smile and checked (in a rather unconvincing manner) that the belts were fastened. I was quite sure that she was laughing to herself about the overdressed fellow beside me.

From the corner of my eye I saw that the woman in the window seat was slyly watching him—a dark haired woman in her forties, clearly well-educated and likely, I thought, to see the comical elements in the linguist's appearance. I, on the other hand, had put a tape into my portable player (remixes of several Miles Davis recordings) and was busy rewinding with my headphones already in place. I gazed along the aisle while I waited for the tape to rewind. All at once I noticed a young, fair-haired woman who was sitting several rows in front of me. I felt as if I recognized her, and when she turned her head towards the person on the other side of the aisle—she had obviously been asked a question—I remembered who she was. I didn't know her name but I had first seen her fifteen years ago, at a high school party in Hjalmholt. Her unconventionally beautiful face had caught my eye, not to mention her almost perfect body, which seemed just the same today.

This memory from Hjalmholt is still very clear, although I was only sixteen or seventeen at the time. There I was sitting on the sofa between two classmates, probably drinking to pluck up enough courage to chat up some girls from my class, and gazing in adoration at this girl I had never seen before but who was, I think, a friend of the people who were throwing the party. It wasn't just her appearance that made her seem exciting; she was even more memorable for having disappeared with a boy, whom I knew vaguely, into one of the children's bedrooms slightly later in the evening. She reappeared half an hour later, red-cheeked and—making no attempt to cover up what she had been doing in the bedroom—with her fair hair tousled (and even prettier), clearly after some kind of "friendly combat," as one of my classmates put it. But the boy, who had gone with her into the bedroom, didn't come out again, and we found out shortly afterwards that he was fast asleep. My friends and I joked that she—the one who was now sitting just a few meters away from me on the plane, in jeans and a T-shirt—had completely done him in.

I never found out any more about this girl—she didn't live in my district nor did she go to the same school as me—but each time I have caught sight of her since then, something begins to happen inside me, something disturbing; I somehow grow smaller and bigger at the same time. In other words: I have fancied her ever since she came out—tousled and flushed, much more mature and exciting than all the other girls—of the children's bedroom. But it's highly unlikely that she remembers me. She left the party soon after she had finished with the boy; she was too smart—too experienced and intelligent—to hang around with children, as I thought my classmates and I were at that time.

Without realizing it, I had begun to compare her beautiful profile (at least what I could see of it from my seat) with that of Vigdis, and, for a few seconds, I seemed to lose my senses; I couldn't remember whether Vigdis had fair or dark hair.

4

The barmaid brought a glass of dark beer and put it on the table for him. She had large breasts, bigger than you would expect on a little body like hers. He gazed at them. He picked up his glass when she put it down on the table and moved it nearer, without taking his eyes off the girl, who turned around and walked back to the bar. Her behind was neat and small compared to her breasts. She took a magazine from the bar, walked behind the counter, and turned up the music. Then she sat down with it, crossed her legs, and began to turn the pages. He carried on looking at her. He lifted his beer glass, put it back down on the table, and dipped his finger in the thick froth. He licked the froth off his finger and groaned. It wasn't easy to guess what emotions the groan was meant to express. The girl seemed to hear him despite the music; she looked at him casually and then turned back to her magazine. After a little while he lifted his glass again and took a long draught. Half the beer had disappeared when he put it down again, wiping the line of froth from his top lip with the back of his hand. When he had swallowed it, he let out a long, loud sounding "ah" and called out to the girl, asking if he could get something to eat here. She said he could; they had sandwiches and soup. He said he wasn't going to have any soup but wouldn't mind a sandwich; what choices did she have? She closed the magazine, stood up without saying a word and brought a menu which she put down on the table. He had finished his beer and passed her the glass in exchange for the menu. She asked if he wanted another one. He nodded and asked for a Jägermeister to go with it, and just some kind of toasted sandwich with ham and cheese. She could put other ingredients in it too, but not asparagus or whatever it was called.

When she had gone off with the glass and the menu, he pulled a pack of cigarettes out of his pocket, tapped out one cigarette, and lit it. The girl brought him the beer and the Jägermeister and then disappeared into the kitchen. He had only had a sip of beer when she came out again with the sandwich, but his schnapps glass was empty. He had taken off his anorak and laid it on the next table. Underneath he was wearing a light yellow shirt and a dark, double-breasted jacket. The barmaid sat down again and carried on looking at her magazine. He gulped down the sandwich and finished off the beer. Just as he was asking the girl to bring him another one, the door opened and a young couple walked in. She was wearing a baggy parka and a dark brown furry hat, while he had on a long overcoat with a strange looking hood. He stood up and asked the girl for another Jägermeister to drink with the beer, then he disappeared into the men's room.

The girl took the drinks to his table and met him as he came out of the toilet. He smiled at her but didn't get a smile back. Then he put on his anorak, picked up the plastic bag, and peered into it to make sure that everything was still in place. He swallowed the schnapps, screwed up his face, as if he was in slight pain, and downed about half the beer in one gulp. He zipped up his anorak, took several steps in the direction of the outside door, looked back towards the kitchen, and then went out. An icy blast blew into the bar, and the door took a good thirty seconds to close again. An uncanny silence fell on the place; the couple at the table stared at the door in wonder, and when the girl came back in from the kitchen he had gone. The only signs of his presence were his half empty beer glass, cigarette stubs in the ashtray, bread crumbs on a plate, and a crumpled napkin.

He now stood with his plastic bag on Hverfisgata, just opposite the Danish Embassy, and looked around several times before he carried on down the street. He walked up Ingolfstraeti and turned down Bankastraeti. The sun began to shine when he got near Laekjargata but had disappeared again behind a cloud by the time he reached the taxi stop below the little old houses of Bernhoftstorfa. He pushed down his hood and squeezed into the first taxi. He didn't answer when the taxi driver commented on how cold the weather had been that month but asked to be driven up to Breidholt, to Sudurholar; probably it was Sudurholar. He would recognize the place when they got there.

5

Armann Valur nudged me with his elbow and placed the open flight magazine on my table, beside the tape player. The German model Claudia Schiffer gazed up at me from the page. I removed one earphone so I could hear what Armann was trying to say. He kept his eyes fixed on the magazine as he tapped the picture of Claudia with his finger. Then, lowering his voice as if he didn't want the woman by the window to hear, he said:

"She's not bad, this one."

I said no in agreement, waited a few seconds before I put the earphone back in place, and sat up straight in my seat, as if to state that I wanted to be left alone. A new track was playing when I started listening again and, as I tend to do when I listen to music, I tried to harmonize it with Claudia's face, which was still gazing at me from the magazine. I could easily imagine the slow, relaxed drum beats of Miles's music being used as background music in a photo studio in Europe while some model shifted positions or pouted and ran her fingers through her golden locks. Vigdis came to mind. At this moment, she was probably changing sheets in the hotel just by the church, and was no doubt wondering if I would call her as soon as I got home, as I had promised. I hadn't made up my mind if I was going to call her straight away or relax and listen to one or two records in the living room first. The only thing I was sure of was that I was looking forward to coming home to my own flat; unpacking the CDs, books, and videos which I had bought; and arranging the wine bottles, cigars, and cigarettes from the duty-free store on the table in the living room. I decided to postpone answering the questions that popped up in my mind: whether Vigdis and I were really in love, or if the exciting feeling I experienced when I imagined her, in a short black skirt, changing sheets in the hotel up north, had anything to do with her personally, or if this imaginary figure could be anyone, even the blonde from Hjalmholt.

Armann didn't seem to have understood that I wanted to be left alone. I had shut my eyes and was trying to look as though I was concentrating on the music in the headphones, but it didn't seem to make any impact on my neighbor; he nudged me again and wanted me to look back at the magazine. On the right-hand page, beside the conclusion of the interview with Claudia, there was an ad showing all kinds of Icelandic products that were ideal to buy for friends and business colleagues abroad: for example Icelandic sweaters, Black Death, cheese, smoked lamb, and, last but not least, Opal lozenges, which was exactly what Armann was trying to draw my attention to. I nodded and wondered whether my fellow passenger—despite his linguistical education—had different values and manners than other people, or if he had suffered some kind of mental breakdown recently. Perhaps his studies had made him strange. I was thankful that at least he didn't smell of alcohol or sweat, as I had feared, but what I found strangest of all was that he didn't seem interested in talking to me. Instead he was trying to get my attention by pointing to something that he obviously wanted me to share with him.

I saw that the woman by the window was watching us and noticed that she had a reddish-purple mark on her neck. It's a hickey, I said to myself. I saw her as an educated woman of around forty who was on the way home after spending a few days with her foreign lover, and who felt no need to cover up the hickey on her neck; on the contrary, she was very happy with it. She would gladly have paid tax on it, if demanded. I tried to imagine her lover, and pictured an Italian or a Greek, a well-built, stocky man in an expensive black suit and a white shirt, with an open neck, revealing the shiny dark hairs on his chest. In other words: the complete opposite of the man who sat between us, and who was, at this moment, probably considering what goods the world of aviation (if one can use such prosaic terms) was offering and if it was necessary (seen from a more general point of view) to conduct all that commerce in the air. I was quite sure that if I gave him the chance the floodgates would burst open and I wouldn't be left in peace for the rest of the trip.

"Maybe this is something one should try," he said. "They are those giant sized packs, much bigger than these here," he added, shaking the half-full box of Opals he had fished up out of his coat pocket with some difficulty—the seat belt was still fastened over his stomach. He didn't offer me a lozenge this time, just helped himself to one and began to tap the box with his index finger while he examined the catalogue more closely.

I tried to imagine what kind of music this overdressed Opal eater listened to at home and came to the conclusion that some sort of learned silence reigned there, broken, at the most, by the evening news and the occasional program on very abstract subject matters. Probably he had never heard anything like the music that was now playing in my headphones: "On the Corner," from 1972 when Armann was somewhere between twenty-five and thirty years old and, no doubt, still a student. I had started to put together a program of music that I would listen to when I got home and emptied my bags. "Lonely Fire" from Big Fun was number one on that list.

6

While the car waited at the traffic lights at the corner of Laekjargata and Hverfisgata, he took a thick old leather-bound book out of the plastic bag, opened it, and gazed at the first page for a few moments. When he closed the book again he stroked it with his hand, put it down on the car seat, and knocked on the hard cover twice with his knuckles. Then he opened up the plastic bag and examined a beautifully carved sailing ship that was wedged into an open wooden box.

Once they reached Saebraut he asked the taxi driver to stop at a store, where he could buy cigarettes. The driver didn't make any comment, just stopped at a drive-in store a little later. While he waited for the cigarettes he put the book back in the plastic bag beside the ship, closed the bag carefully, and put it down on the seat.

They set off again along Saebraut in the direction of Breidholt. When they were about to turn into Vesturberg he stopped the driver and told him to carry on until they reached a certain block of flats in

the Sudurholar area. He explained to him that he was going to check
if his friend was at home and he wanted the driver to wait. The driver
asked him to leave the plastic bag in the car. He asked the driver if
he didn't trust him and the latter replied that that wasn't the issue, no
one got out of his car without paying. He said OK but how could he
trust the driver, he could just drive away, maybe his wallet was in the
bag—besides the contents of the bag were worth more than a taxi fare,
considerably more. The driver kept silent. He lifted the bag and gave it
a shake, as if he was demonstrating that it was a token of mutual trust,
then he put it down on the seat again and got out of the car.

He ran up the steps which led to the balconies on the second floor,
a sort of outdoor staircase, from which one had access to the flats in
the building. He stopped for a moment outside the second door from
the end but didn't knock, then he went on to the furthest apartment
and rang the bell. A young woman came to the door. She was wearing
a long black T-shirt and tight leggings. He said good morning and
asked if Hinrik, his old pal Rikki, was at home. The woman ran her
eyes up his body and shook her head, he was at work. Then he asked
if Rikki was no longer playing in a band, he had expected him to be
at home in the morning, but the woman repeated that he was at work,
he only played on weekends now. She was getting cold standing in the
doorway and was about to shut the door. He stopped her by putting his
palm up in the air, gave a quick glance back towards the taxi in the
parking lot below, and asked if he could use her toilet. He explained
that he was in a taxi and needed to pee before he set off again. The
woman looked him straight in the face, then lowered her gaze and
looked away before she asked how he knew Hinrik, she wasn't used to
letting strangers in. He said then that they were old friends, he had
even come here before, maybe she didn't remember him but he had
been there just the same, though it could have been before she met
Hinrik. She repeated that she didn't like letting strangers in but gave
in when he pointed to the taxi waiting for him. He was on his way
back downtown.

She stepped back into the hall to let him pass, and he nodded,
stepped in, and offered to take off his shoes. She told him not to bother,
it wasn't necessary, but he said he didn't want to leave dirty footprints.

She told him where to find the toilet, he had to go along the corridor there and it was the middle door.

He disappeared into the bathroom and shut the door. Then he raised the toilet seat and looked in the mirror above the sink. He ran his fingers through his thick hair and noticed that the mirror was the door to a cupboard. He opened the cupboard and looked at the selection of perfume, aftershave, toothbrushes, and medicine. He took out a plastic container of codeine, flicked off the lid, sniffed the contents and stuffed four pills into the breast pocket of his jacket. He ran his finger over other pill jars in the cupboard and before he closed the door he shook a little aftershave into his hand and patted it on to his cheeks and neck. Next he unzipped the fly of his pants, pulled out his penis, and let the dark stream pour straight down like a waterfall into the toilet bowl. He said out loud that was good, as always; there wasn't much that could compete with it. Then in a lower voice, almost whispering, he added: "Especially in strange houses."

7

The captain's voice introduced itself over the loudspeaker. To begin with it sounded as if he was only going to chat to the passengers, but then he began to relate various facts concerning the flight, for instance that we were flying over Scotland, at a height of thirty thousand feet and there were twenty-five degrees of frost outside.

"That's not very warm," Armann commented. Yet I sensed that he was quite happy with the temperature in these parts, besides it was in keeping with the clothes he was wearing. "What would that be in Fahrenheit?" he added.

I told him I didn't know, maybe about twice as high, and at that moment Armann grabbed the opportunity that I was afraid he had been waiting for. He had caught me in a trap that I wouldn't be able to get out of for the rest of the trip.

"Yes, but that is just it," he said and stuffed the Opal box back in his breast pocket, this time so it would be easier to pull out again. "Shouldn't one say 'twice as *low*'? That's the thing with frost and heat;

as soon as the frost increases the heat goes down, isn't that so?"

I felt like telling him to discuss it with the captain but refrained. It wasn't such a terrific sacrifice spending three hours of one's lifetime on something in which one hadn't the slightest interest. I reminded myself that what doesn't kill a man should harden him, and with that in mind I launched into the discussion on frost and temperature, but said I hadn't given it much thought, at least not specifically.

"It is exactly one of the things we make mistakes about," Armann said. I expected him to pass me his Opal box. "In reality the cold never goes up." When he had uttered these words, he bent forward a little and glanced at me, as if he was trying to judge my level of intelligence or observation.

"Really?" I asked dubiously, and consoled myself with the thought that it took much less energy participating in something boring than trying to struggle against it, especially when there was no possibility of avoiding it.

"Yes, it is just like that," Armann said and raised his index finger to emphasize the point. "Heat rises on the other hand. When there are heat waves old people die in their cars, even people my age—except, of course, I don't have a car—but as soon as one moves to a colder part of the world, as for instance where we are now, the situation is reversed: the cold actually goes down as the frost hardens."

"No, are you sure about that?" I interrupted. I thought it rather unlikely that he really believed what he was stating.

"Yes," he said, but he took time to reconsider his earlier statement. "What I mean is that the more degrees of frost that are added, the lower the heat goes, and as a result the temperature goes down. In other words: the frost goes down."

I was going to object but decided to see just how he would get himself out of this dilemma. I gave him my full attention to show him I expected an explanation.

"We can take a clear example from everyday life," he continued and it was quite obvious that he was waiting impatiently for the flight attendant, who had started to serve drinks, to reach us. "Let's imagine a particular person, one man in a two-room flat. Another man comes in the door and the number of persons in the flat goes up; the number of inhabitants increases but the space allotted to each one diminishes, that is if we imagine that both of them are going to live in the flat."

"Now wait a minute."

"Otherwise they aren't inhabitants, as we understand the word," he added hastily.

"I wasn't referring to that."

"Let's just imagine that these two individuals have bought the flat together. They were maybe inclined that way, if you know what I mean."

"But you are talking about two completely different concepts," I said. "Numbers and space. One can't compare numbers and space, especially when you are trying to support your proposition that cold can't go up, just go down."

I thought that he would begin to realize the frivolity of the conversation and give up. But he stubbornly carried on.

"Yes, you can," he said, "just as hot and cold are completely different concepts. It's feasible that there are no other entities in the world as strongly opposed as heat and cold. One goes up while the other goes down."

"Not at the same time," I objected. "Though the temperature goes up somewhere, that doesn't mean that the cold goes down at the same time. Unless you mean that while the heat goes up in Bolivia, for example, there will be more frost in Norway, or something like that."

"That is just what I mean," Armann replied, very pleased with himself. "Just like the example with the flat; the greater the number of inhabitants the less space there will be." His serious expression—and the pause in his argument—hinted that we had reached a certain level of agreement in our discussion, "a certain landing," if one could talk in those terms. But, even though the discussion had come to a close, I couldn't resist adding one more comment.

"But the temperature goes down too," I said and emphasized the word *down*.

"Is that so?" Armann said. I couldn't make out whether his question revealed his lack of interest or lack of confidence.

"You can't deny it," I said.

"Only up to a certain level," he answered. "When the temperature is so low that it reaches freezing point, then it begins to . . ." He hesitated, and, in order to gain time to think, he waved to the flight attendant, who was still too far away to be of any assistance.

I, for my part, began to wonder, as a result of our conversation, what decision the captain would take when the plane approached Keflavik airport. Would he go up or down? Would we, Armann and I, and the rest of the passengers, succeed in landing?

8

When he emerged from the bathroom, he stayed on the threshold for a little while, lifted his hands up to his face to sniff them, then took hold of the doorknob without turning around, and quietly closed the door. He looked about for the woman, but when he didn't catch sight of her, he went into the next room. The door was partly open, and, after giving it a gentle push, it revealed a child's bedroom. He smiled and looked around the colorful little room; it was full of toddlers' toys which were jumbled together with things that belonged to a slightly older child, obviously a boy. Then he walked over to a small desk with a computer on top. The computer seemed to be too big for the table; there wasn't room for anything else on it. He pressed a letter on the keyboard and a soldier in a camouflage uniform—holding a big machine gun, with a helmet on his head and a fierce, pitiless expression on his face—popped up. He was startled. He jerked his hands back and shook them, like he was also holding a vibrating machine gun, though he didn't add the appropriate sound effects. Then he tapped the computer, as if he was patting a child on the head, before turning to the large birdcage beside the desk.

There were two little budgies in the cage. He bent down to it, tapped on the rails, and clicked with his tongue in an attempt to attract their attention. The birds just looked at him, nothing more; they seemed completely uninterested. He picked up a yellow pencil which was lying on the desk beside the computer, poked it carefully in between the bars of the cage, and waggled it, but the birds took no notice. So he poked the pencil into the stomach of one of the birds. That resulted in both of them flying up with loud squawks; they seemed to crash into each other or the sides of the cage. It was difficult to see exactly what they were doing, but the noise they produced brought Hinrik's frightened wife running into the room and she asked him what on earth was going on. He answered that he had unexpectedly found himself in this room; he had no doubt gone in the wrong direction when he came out of the bathroom. The birds seemed to have calmed down.

The woman directed him out into the hall. While he followed her, he praised the child for his attractive bedroom, or were there perhaps two children, he had noticed that there were bunks in the room. At least they were animal lovers, it was years since he had seen a budgie in a cage. She didn't reply, just waited by the hall door with her arms crossed. He walked into the hall, and when he bent over his shoes he seemed to remember something suddenly. He straightened up and asked the woman if he could make one phone call, he needed to see if another friend of his was at home before he set off again in the taxi. She sighed impatiently, said something about it being quite sufficient that he had been allowed to use the toilet, she wasn't sure that it was normal allowing some stranger to come in, he must be able to understand that. He said he did, of course she should never open the door to a stranger, but, as he and Rikki were such good friends, she could trust him one hundred percent. It was obvious from the expression on the woman's face that she didn't quite know how she should react to this last comment, but after thinking a little, staring worriedly at the floor, and puffing as if she was exhaling cigarette smoke, she gave in and said he could make one call, but it had to be short. She was busy, had no time for this. He thanked her.

As he picked up the receiver, he called out to her that he just had to dial information first; he wasn't quite sure of the number. When he got through to the operator, he asked for the number of Emil S. Halldorsson, Grettisgata something or other, he wasn't quite sure what the number was. While he was pressing the numbers that he had been given, there was a loud knock on the front door and the woman went to answer it, swearing under her breath that there was no peace here at home, during lunchtime in the middle of the week. The cab driver stood on the doorstep and asked the woman politely if his passenger was by any chance still inside. She said he was coming, he was just making a phone call.

He had let the phone ring for a good while without getting any reply, and when he came back and saw the taxi driver in the doorway, he smiled and said well, well, so he had come to fetch him. The driver said he had just wanted to check if he had disappeared off the face of the earth. While he put on his shoes he thanked the woman warmly, he had expected such kindness from the wife of his friend Hinrik, who was such a fine fellow. His last words were that no one had answered at his friend's house, he was no doubt working, just like poor old Rikki, and then he followed the driver down to the parking lot. Once inside the car, he said he wanted to go down to Austurstraeti, where the driver would be rid of him. He wouldn't have to worry about him any more, at least not for the rest of that day. He took the leather-bound book out of the plastic bag and was busy turning over the pages as the taxi drove out of the car park and along the road.

9

Probably half an hour had passed since take-off. The woman in the window seat asked the flight attendant for two little bottles of white wine and said no thank you when she was offered a liqueur to have with her coffee later. I had made up my mind not to drink anything on the way; I was going to wait until the evening when my friends, Saebjorn and Jaime, were going to drop in. Those plans were altered when Armann ordered four little bottles of red wine and told the flight attendant to put two of them on my table. I didn't want to decline his offer, and after a few minutes' thought—which involved changing my plans for the rest of the day—I decided to take an active part in the wine purchasing by ordering four miniature bottles of Cointreau to have with our coffee; two for me and two for Armann. He seemed really pleased at that. But later it became apparent that the red wine was free—part of the service, Armann said with a smug smile, rephrasing the information he'd been given by the flight attendant—while I needed to pay for the liqueurs with my credit card, which I had to fetch from the overhead bin. While I was standing up, Armann turned to the woman in the window seat and asked her if we couldn't offer her a liqueur with her coffee. By using the word *we* he had made us into comrades. She thanked Armann for the offer but no, she wasn't very partial to strong drinks. Armann seemed almost offended when she declined; he repeated what she had said, "not partial to strong drinks," and when I sat down again I heard him mumble something to the effect that it was her choice.

"These bottles don't hold much," he observed and lifted one of the red wine bottles up to eye-level. "Perhaps it's about one glassful. Maybe slightly more."

I replied that he was probably right but didn't want to say any more, in case he was going to start another discussion like the one on heat and cold. Armann opened the bottle he was holding, poured the contents into his glass, and then put his hand into his inner coat pocket and pulled out a paperback. I couldn't imagine him shutting himself off in a book and, of course, that was not quite what he had in mind. He opened the book and while he turned the pages (rather roughly for my liking) he said he wanted to show me something. He had bought this book in Foyles Bookshop on Charing Cross Road and discovered, afterwards really, that it was exactly what he had been looking for.

"That was lucky," I said and poured red wine into my glass.

"Yes, you could definitely say that," Armann answered. "It's always a pleasure when life takes one by surprise. It doesn't happen that often, does it?"

He pulled his glasses case out of his jacket pocket. Like the Opal box, it appeared to have been sat on. However, I was rather surprised at how modern the shape of the frames were, and I noticed that the woman by the window watched Armann's clumsy movements—he put on his glasses and replaced the case in his pocket—with a smile. He seemed to be having trouble finding what he was going to show me, and the woman, who had taken out *Harper's Bazaar* from her bag, appeared to be rather shocked at the way Armann thumbed his way back and forth through his book. She, on the other hand, turned the pages so carefully that I imagined she had bought the magazine for someone else at home and wanted it to look untouched.

I asked Armann what the title of the book was.

"It's a really remarkable volume," he said, but was too engrossed in

turning the pages to answer my question. I hadn't noticed what was on
the cover but from the little diagrams—some kind of calculations with
words instead of numbers—I guessed that it was of a scientific nature,
no doubt some complicated, advanced grammatical text.

Although I didn't expect to have peace for long, I used the opportunity to replace my headphones and switched on Miles again. The
fair-haired girl in the T-shirt was resting her bare elbow on the armrest,
her head leaning to one side as she gazed along the aisle. She had her
index finger on her cheek and let her fourth finger play with her lips as
if she was deep in thought over what she saw. I couldn't see if she was
drinking anything but imagined she had white wine like the woman
beside Armann. I thought it was very likely that she was traveling
alone; I hadn't seen her talk to anyone except the flight attendant and
the person on the other side of the aisle.

I looked at her for quite a while and began to wonder how long I
could carry on gazing without her being aware of me. No doubt, she
knew already. I think I always notice when someone is watching me;
it doesn't matter whether the person is sitting beside me or is further
away.

All at once I felt Armann nudge me gently with his elbow. At the
same moment the fair-haired girl turned round, as if she had heard
something further back in the plane. Our eyes met for a moment. She
had clearly begun to smell the food, which I also smelled now as the
trolley came nearer, but, though our gazes had met, it was impossible
to say if she had noticed me.

I took off the headphones to attend to Armann.

"See here," he said. He held up the book and pointed with a thick,
short finger at the upper right hand page.

"What?"

"Look."

"What is it?" I asked, my mind still on the fair-haired girl.

Armann tapped the tape player on my table and then pointed at the
text in the book. He read out:

"Since the Sony Walkman was introduced, no one has been sure
whether two of them should be *Walkmen* or *Walkmans*." He looked at
me and asked if I had ever considered it.

I shook my head.

Then he carried on: "(The nonsexist alternative), that's in brackets here," he added, "(The nonsexist alternative *Walkpersons* would leave us on the hook, because we would be faced with a choice between *Walkpersons* and *Walkpeople*)." He stopped reading out loud but stared at the page as if he was still reading silently. He nodded, looked at me and then at the educated woman, no doubt hoping that she was listening too.

"That's a question," he said.

"Yes, it is a question," I agreed and took the tape out of my Walkman, not to turn it round but just to keep my hands occupied.

Armann took a good sip of red wine before he continued, and as I picked up my glass to keep him company the woman at the window did exactly the same, although she didn't seem to be aware that we were drinking simultaneously.

"That's the crux of the matter," Armann said. "They produce one instrument, for example this one here," he tapped my player again, "but as soon as they use technology to produce a second player and then number three and so on, they no longer know what to call their invention in the plural. They are faced with a grammatical problem that no instrument has been invented to solve. Of course it is the same dilemma that parents have to cope with when they give birth to twins or triplets. Really they should all have the same name, that is if they are identical and the same sex; they come one after another from the same producer, they are as identical inwardly as two such instruments from Sony and the only thing that differentiates them is—at least superficially—the same thing which differentiates one Sony instrument from another."

At this point he paused and looked at me over his glasses; he obviously expected me to be keen to find out what it was that differentiated one instrument from another.

"What can that be?" I asked.

"What differentiates identical twins is the treatment they receive, at least how they are treated as children and teenagers; what they are fed, what noises, words and music they hear. In other words: upbringing. I don't mean just musical upbringing, rather upbringing in general, which I have always thought should be called treatment."

"Isn't that too clinical a word?"

"Treatment?" He almost seemed to snort at my comment. "It could well be that it is clinical but I think it is more suitable to express up-bringing, at least from a general point of view. Most children are of course not brought up in any way, instead they just undergo some sort of treatment from their parents. Naturally, the treatment varies, but quite a few of them simply just get such rough treatment that they will never be anything else but children. I know about that."

He paused again and in the meantime I imagined that something had gone wrong in his upbringing, something that he realized had had an effect on him as an adult. Then he carried on:

"But whatever happened; if you had an identical twin brother, which I doubt you have, then he should really be called . . .?"

It took me a few seconds to realize that I was being asked a question.

"Emil," I said. Just as I had expected, he didn't remember my name.

"Emil. Yes, that's as good a name as any. Emil Jonsson."

"Emil Halldorsson," I corrected him. "Emil S. Halldorsson."

"You know who Emil Jonsson was, don't you?"

"Can't say I do," I answered.

"It can be useful to know about famous people who share your name," he said and sat up straight in his seat. "Emil Jonsson is not the worst namesake one could think of, I am quite sure of that."

"I don't think I have ever heard him mentioned," I said, and it oc-curred to me to mention my namesake in the Swedish Smålands, but I changed my mind.

"But perhaps you are no better off knowing about someone who bore your name in the past," Armann carried on. "Least of all if he is dead."

For a moment I wondered whether my namesake, whom I had thought of mentioning, was still alive or not, and whether characters in stories grew old in the same way as, for example, their authors.

"But you aren't a twin, are you?" Armann asked. He smiled and waited for my answer, as if he wanted to make sure that I had come into this world alone, was one of a kind and so on.

I said I wasn't.

"Consider yourself lucky," he said.

"What do you mean?"

"Not to be a twin."

This last comment made me think that he was hinting at his own personal experience of being a twin (could he even be an identical twin?), and yet it was unthinkable that there could be another version of such a man.

"Then it mentions slightly further on," he went on and turned over the page of the book. "It states here: 'Fearing that their trademark, if converted to a noun, may become as generic as *aspirin* or *kleenex*, they,' that is Sony, of course, 'sidestep the grammatical issues by insisting upon *Walkman Personal Stereos.*' In other words they avoid the issue by removing the grammar from the name of the instrument. Or the name of the technology, to be more exact."

"Is that so?" I said. "The company directors have started controlling how we talk?"

"There is no question about it," Armann answered, clearly very happy that I showed interest in the subject. "They cut out the grammar in the name of their product because they don't have a good enough grasp of language. One who knows that he is in the wrong naturally tries to convince everyone else that he is in the right; that is usually the way that information is passed on from man to man. They can produce an instrument that enables you to enjoy your favorite songs at thirty thousand feet above sea-level but when it comes to giving this remarkable instrument a name, they haven't the ability to name more than a single copy; all the other copies are left in some problematic limbo. People all over the world who own the instruments are totally helpless because they don't know how to name them when someone asks. But there is also the other possibility: that each copy is different."

He fell silent at this point, as if he was giving me the chance to say something. Then he asked for my opinion.

"On what?" I asked.

"Whether each copy could be different?"

"That's a question," I said, and I realized as soon as I had said it that I had answered with this phrase before. It looked as if I had only one response on hand in reply to what the linguist was telling me and that answer had to include the word *question*.

"But I personally don't believe that each individual product of this kind is unique," he continued and pointed again at my tape player. "Isn't it made somewhere in East Asia? Where everyone is virtually the same, whether he works with a conveyor belt or at a desk or stoops half starved over some paddy field?"

I said I thought it was produced in Korea or Japan and restrained myself from objecting to his statement that all the inhabitants of these countries were the same.

"However it may well be that they are all individual," he said, as if he regretted having clumsily exposed his antipathy for Asians. "Maybe it's possible to find some minute differences between one Japanese and another. But then we can also consider the opposite of Japanese technology: the Russian automobile industry! No two vehicles are the same. Each Lada, Moskvitch, or whatever it is called, is absolutely unique. Of course the Russian car comes into existence in a similar manner as most babies do, that is to say under the influence of alcohol or drugs."

Suddenly he pushed his nose up in the air and sniffed. Then he looked back towards the flight attendant, who was approaching with the food trays, and said:

"It seems as though they are going to treat us to something."

It flashed through my mind that Armann Valur could be as much under the influence as the Russian mechanics allegedly were. I thought it unlikely that the half glass of red wine he had drunk could stimulate those weird speculations on tape players and the book from Foyles. Not to mention the subject he moved on to next: that his favorite word was *limbo*. He felt that he, personally, was often in some kind of limbo, both in respect to his life as a human being, that is the *life pattern*—as he expressed it—and his life as a thinking individual amongst other thinking individuals, and often individuals who didn't seem to think very much at all from one minute to the next. But whatever the outcome, and maybe exactly because of these thoughts of his, I was beginning to enjoy Armann's company—even though he was certainly one of those personalities one would never wish to have as a lifelong acquaintance or consider inviting home.

The aroma of the food seemed to have taken complete control of Armann and he had definitely lost all interest in those forms of research into which he had been giving me glimpses. He managed to stuff the book back into his pocket with a certain amount of difficulty—although it was a paperback it was too big for an average sized pocket—and he got ready for the meal by putting the flight magazine back in the seat pocket, brushing something off the sleeve of his overcoat and rubbing his hands together, like someone who is looking forward to something good. Next he took off his glasses and put them down on the table, which was ready for the food tray.

I guessed we would get chicken.

10

The cab driver pulled up in the parking space in front of the ice cream stand at Ingolfstorg. He paid the driver and when he told him to keep the four hundred kronur change, the driver, who hadn't uttered a word all the way, said he never took more than the rate; he pointed at the meter and said that was the price, that was what he accepted for the ride. Then it will just have to be danger money, he said as he opened the door and worked his way out. He shut the door behind him, zipped up his anorak, fitted his hood over his head, and walked into Austurstraeti with his plastic bag. When he had gone several meters along the street he suddenly turned round and went back in the direction of the square. The taxi was still in the parking lot, and he knocked on passenger's side window as he passed by. The driver seemed startled; he watched his former passenger walk on, and then muttered something under his breath when he saw the passenger stop at the ice cream stand and talk to a young man.

He asked for ice cream with a topping. Wasn't it possible to have it hot, it was so bloody cold outside. The young man smiled and said he could make him a child-size ice cream, he would be quicker with it. Maybe that was the thing, he answered; he'd have a child's size one. Children knew what they wanted; if anyone could make a right decision it was a child. When he took the chocolate-covered cornet (and looked goggle-eyed at it, amazed at how small it was) he asked the youth if he knew of any good bars in the vicinity, if there were any in

Austurstraeti for instance. Yes, there were two or three in Austurstraeti, but there were more and rather better ones in the neighboring streets— the ones on Austurstraeti were pretty weird. There was one that was some kind of health bar and another very strange one on the right—he gave more accurate details on how to find it—but wasn't quite sure whether he should recommend going there. He liked the sound of it and would take a look at the strange place. The young man asked him if he had come from the country and he replied that he had been in Breidholt. Then he smiled, pierced the crisp chocolate with his teeth, and took a large bite. With his mouth full, he told the young man he had been living abroad, hadn't been in Reykjavik for several years. He swallowed the ice cream and gave a shudder, it was so cold, then added that he was just visiting an old friend before going abroad again. He paid for the ice cream, said he was going to take a look at this strange bar, and got a peculiar smile from the young man behind the counter.

He walked straight over to the bar, as if he knew exactly where it was. He peered through the window before going in and dropped the half-eaten cornet on to the pavement. He stood on it and squashed it like he was putting out a cigarette.

Inside the bar, three men were sitting at a table beside the counter and a man and a woman were at another table near the window. The smell in there was the smell of yesterday, or all the yesterdays that had been since it opened—stale cigarette smoke that seemed somehow to choke any possibility of good memories. The interior was clearly not designed to distract attention from the customers, who all looked as if they had been there a long time. But, despite the fact that he had just come in, they took no special interest in him. He walked up to the bar and asked for a double vodka and coffee, if there was any coffee to be had. The bartender was a man of about fifty, with bushy eyebrows and a thick mustache. There was no coffee ready but he could make some; he, the bartender—who seemed to be the owner of the place—had coffee, that was no problem, he'd see to it straight away.

The three men who sat beside the bar had clearly become interested in his conversation with the bartender; they turned round to face the bar and one of them, who seemed to be the oldest, or at least had sat there longer than the others, said the word coffee, as if it hadn't been heard in there before. Then they carried on talking and suddenly, in the blink of an eye, they were quarreling noisily, so loudly that the bartender ordered them to shut up or they would have to leave. They calmed down quickly, almost as though someone had blinked again.

He took the vodka glass and sat down at a table in the middle of the place but he stood up again straight away and asked the bartender, who was busy making coffee, if he could make a phone call. The men at the table looked at him again in wonder. He was shown into a room behind the bar that seemed to serve both as a wine cellar and the kitchen. There were several framed prints on one of the walls—they reminded him of the inside of a retired sailors' home—as well as two pin-up pictures from porn magazines. One showed a pale woman of about fifty, who had remarkably firm breasts for her age. He gazed at the picture while he called information and asked for the number of Emil Halldorsson, Emil S. Halldorsson. While he held the receiver in his left hand and waited for the number, he grabbed hold of his crotch with his right hand, rubbing and pressing the denim with his thumb. He let go of himself when he got the number, transferred the receiver to his right hand, and called again. Like when he called from Sudurholar, no one answered.

When he came back out into the smoke-filled air in the bar he smelled the aroma of brewing coffee and stopped to breathe it in. Havard sat down again beside the vodka glass and had a swig. He was just about to light a cigarette when one of the three men by the bar spoke to him: Hey, you there, you got a special contract already? Laughter rose up around the table and was followed by a bad fit of coughing from one of them, who had a particularly pale face. Another, the only one who sat facing him, told him not to take any notice of his friend, he hadn't woken up yet; he had no idea what he was saying. But he wanted to know what the man had meant when he asked if he had a special contract. The one who had spoken didn't seem to be in any state to explain, he was too busy coughing, but his friend told him not to worry, it was nothing. Then he slapped the weakling on the back and stuck a cigarette in his mouth, as if to glue his lips together. The latter dragged out the cigarette, laughed wheezily while he got over his coughing fit, put the cigarette back between his lips, and lit it. Then he took out a leather wallet from the inside pocket of his jacket and pulled out several kronur bills. He counted the money, returned it to his wallet, and put the wallet back into his pocket. The way he behaved suggested that he was in the habit of counting his money quite regularly. The newcomer stood up from his table, picked up his empty vodka glass, and walked up to the bar. The owner of the place, who had just poured steaming coffee into a cup for him, automatically brought out the vodka bottle, poured some into the empty glass, and asked if he needed milk or sugar in his coffee. He said no, turned around, and went up the table where the three men sat. He stood still for a little while, staring directly at the one who had just finished counting the money in his wallet. All three of the men stared back at him. Their expressions suggested that they had seen something unexpected; something was about to happen, and they would have to react.

11

After the meal, which turned out to be some kind of Cordon Bleu and not chicken as I had guessed, Armann fell asleep with his empty food tray in front of him. He had declined the flight attendant's offer of coffee, finished off his red wine and one of the Cointreau bottles, and nodded off almost before he had swallowed it. The flight attendant suggested that I tip his seat back, so that he would be more comfortable. While I was adjusting Armann's seat, the woman by the window asked me, with a slightly mocking expression on her face, if I was going to cover him up with a rug too. I smiled back and said I thought he was wrapped up well enough already. She looked as though she was going to try to fall asleep too, and when she had shut her eyes, with her head resting against the window of the plane, I imagined that she was tired after spending last night with her lover and was floating into sleep on those memories. Now, when it was nearly three o'clock and one hour into this three hour flight.

On the other hand, it was impossible to say what was going on in Armann's mind. At first I thought of him having fallen asleep like a little child, but after further reflection I decided it was inappropriate;

one would never see this kind of expression on a child's face, even if its parents had poked it for fun or pulled its skin this way and that. Sleep would never disfigure a face so badly, except perhaps on a person who always slept alone and didn't have to think day and night of looking good for a wife or lover. I smiled at this poor theory of mine—I began to wonder if I had been infected by my fellow passenger's lively imagination—but I only needed to look over to the other side of the aisle to realize that there might be some truth in it. A middle-aged couple, who had asked me earlier to help them get their luggage down from the overhead bin, were asleep, and there was such a childlike, peaceful expression on the man's face that it was impossible to imagine he had ever frowned, or looked depraved or lustful, even when he was enjoying intercourse with his wife.

"May I take the tray?" the flight attendant asked.

I was going to pass her the woman's tray first. She seemed to be asleep, but then I saw she hadn't touched the dessert, so I offered to lift Armann's tray instead—he had clearly enjoyed all the food. But in order to get the tray off the table I had to be rather organized; he had put his glasses down in his unused coffee cup and his right hand—with three fingers gripping the tray, as if to prevent it from being thrown away—lay in his lap, heavy with sleep. I managed to loosen his fingers and move his hand without waking him. I couldn't think where to put his glasses while I helped the flight attendant, so I pushed them into the pocket of my shirt and got rid of our used food trays.

Once the food trays have been removed, one feels that a very important stage has been reached. Besides having been fed and feeling comfortably full, the second stage of the journey has begun, or is about to at least, and then there's not so long to wait until one can fill one's lungs with, on the one hand, desperately wanted cigarette smoke and, on the other hand, cold fresh air, at least if one is on the way, as we were, to Iceland from abroad.

The flight attendant thanked me for helping her with the trays and offered me more coffee. I accepted and added what was left of the first liqueur bottle to it.

Vigdis came to mind. When I called her from the hotel the day before yesterday she said she would call me from Akureyri after I got

home, though she wasn't quite sure when. She was going to be at a
meeting which could last all evening. She had asked me to buy her a
jumper and some pants from a certain shop on Oxford Street; I didn't
find them, despite looking for an hour yesterday on my last trip to the
shops. She had also told me to buy some special make of clothes for
Halldor, my son, but I hadn't had time to find them either. I bought
a computer game instead, and I was already beginning to worry that
it would be outdated by the time he came to visit me from Denmark
in May or June. As I hadn't bought anything for Vigdis I was going
to get some perfume or sweets for her in the duty-free store and find
some clothes for her later on Laugavegur; I wouldn't see her before next
weekend at the earliest anyway.

Armann and the woman by the window were both sleeping soundly.
I was wide awake and stood up to go to the toilet, though I didn't have
any great need to go. One of the toilets was out of order—there was a
hand-written sign—and I stood behind a young man who was waiting
for the other one. The flight attendant, who had freed me of the food
trays, was filling up the wine supplies on her trolley in the space beyond
the toilets. She smiled at me and asked if I wanted more to drink with
my coffee. I said no thank you, I had enough for the time being. Then
I sensed that someone had joined the line, and, on turning around, I
came eye to eye with the blonde from Hjalmholt. Before I turned back
again she seemed to screw up her face, as if she had an itch or was
trying to move her glasses further up her nose, although she wasn't
wearing any. The man in front of me was becoming impatient. He
muttered something under his breath. The flight attendant thought he
was talking to her, and he asked grumpily if she couldn't find a plumber
amongst the passengers. I turned to the girl.

"This is going to take some time," I said cheerfully and tried not to
let the man in front hear me.

"I've plenty of time," she answered with a smile.

Of course people have enough time onboard airplanes; they have
far too much time. I couldn't think of anything more to say to improve
on the clumsy remark I had made, but she came to my rescue by filling
the silence:

"Can you imagine what went wrong in the other toilet?"

"I'm doing my best not to," I said, rather pleased with myself for this answer. The fact that I was standing here in the aisle of the airplane talking to this beautiful woman, whom I had kept in the back of my mind for fifteen years, made me feel like I was in some kind of romantic comedy—the kind of film I usually try to avoid, though in this case I must admit that I wanted it to continue and reach a conclusion I had already started to hope for. "But I am beginning to wonder if something has happened in this one as well," I added.

"They are dangerous places, these toilets," the blonde said. "I think I'll mess my pants in a minute."

I didn't quite know quite what to reply to this, if she really meant what she was saying.

"There is an even longer line at the other end of the plane," she continued. "I don't know what's going on; maybe there was something in the food."

"You can go before me," I said, trying to sound as if I wasn't doing her any special favor. "That's if the person inside ever comes out."

"Can I?" she said, gratefully, and just then a middle-aged woman came out of the toilet with a small child.

"No problem," I said. "I can wait."

She thanked me and when the woman and child had gone back to their seats, and the man in front had disappeared into the toilet, she said she knew what it was like with children. It took twice as long to help them though they were half our size. We didn't say any more before she went in, but I couldn't help imagining what she was doing once she had disappeared inside the plastic door and bolted the lock. I was in no hurry to get to the toilet and I rather hoped that she would take her time. I enjoyed standing there, making sure that no one disturbed her.

"It's alright for you to enter," she said with a smile when she came out, but I was partly wishing that she had left some kind of smell behind. Then she thanked me, and as she walked off in the direction of her seat, I noticed that she was carrying a little toilet bag.

I'm not sure if I imagined it but I felt as if she had given me some kind of signal with her eyes when she smiled at me. I was quite certain I wouldn't be able to shake this woman out of my mind straight away.

There was a rather heavy, heady perfume floating in the air that appealed to me straight away; she had brought her perfume in her toilet bag and had decided to use it after our conversation.

She looked back at me once, later on in the flight, and we smiled politely at each other.

Armann didn't wake up until the captain announced that we were descending and that there were fourteen degrees of frost in Keflavik. Several passengers shivered at the very thought of it. But Armann didn't seem to be very cold, he had clearly sweated while he slept, and I noticed that the woman by the window, who had just woken up too, couldn't help smiling when she saw the beads of perspiration on the forehead of this overdressed man.

Armann didn't say a word until we were just about to touch down. Then he suddenly started talking, and it was quite obvious that he was nervous. Out of the blue he began to tell me about a bartender he had met in his hotel in London. He had been chatting to him late one evening and the bartender—who had the same surname as both the Prime Minister of England and the author of Animal Farm (that is, before he assumed his "nom de plume")—had told him a little story that explained why he had turned to heavy drinking and smoking as a young man. One of his teachers in secondary school had been a strict teetotaler, and just before he bade farewell to his pupils, who were going off to grapple with life or on to other educational institutions, he wanted to show them once and for all the destructive nature of alcohol and tobacco. He placed three glasses of water on his desk, and added alcohol to the first and nicotine to the second, leaving the third uncontaminated, just pure water.

"If one can talk about pure water in England," Armann added in an aside.

Then the teacher opened a little cardboard box, and pulled out a black insect, which was about the size of a cigarette filter, with a pair of tweezers.

By now the airplane had come to a halt and people had started to pull down their belongings from the overhead bins. I asked Armann to excuse me while I got down my bag and, because I didn't want to block the flow of passengers on the way to the exit, I tried to signal to him that I had to leave without hearing the rest of the story. Armann had also stood up and wiped his hand across his sweaty brow. Though he was well into his story about the bartender, he still looked rather sleepy and it was obvious that he wasn't enjoying this part of the journey very much.

12

The bartender seemed to be keeping a close eye on what was happening at the table. No sooner had he said, "For God's sake, let's have no trouble," than a hand gripped the shoulder of the man who had mentioned the contract and pulled him out of his seat. The cigarette fell from his hand and it was difficult to see what upset his companions more: the hot ashes that scattered over the table or the assault. The pale, sickly fellow was shaken about for several seconds, as if the ground under his feet was rocked by sharp tremors, and then his companions stood up to help him; one of them—the one who had tried to explain that his friend was in a bad way—was quick to act, but the other, who had obviously drunk more than the rest of them, took longer to heave his body up off the chair. The man who now held the weakling by the shoulders, dragged him towards the door and, before his mates had time to come to his rescue, slipped his hand into the inner jacket pocket and snatched out the tattered wallet. He then gave the man a push in the direction of his friends, which caused him to slump down in a heap at their feet. He grabbed hold of the plastic bag that he had kept on his table, ran to the door, and was out on the pavement before anyone could do anything. When the three comrades emerged a few seconds later and began to quarrel about the direction in which the damned fellow had gone, he had disappeared round the corner of Austurstraeti and Posthusstraeti. He dropped the wallet into the plastic bag and ran on in the direction of Hotel Borg. There was no sign that anyone had noticed him. When he had gotten as far as the alleyway behind the hotel he stopped, got his breath back, and spat on the pavement, as if he were getting rid of something that had been afflicting him for a long time. He looked inside the plastic bag and checked that he had everything:

the book, the sailing ship, and the wallet. He then gave a sigh of relief
and took a few minutes to gaze at a sculpture which depicted either a
business man holding on to a briefcase, with the top half of his body
enclosed in a large square stone block, or a large, walking stone block,
with arms and a briefcase in one hand. He looked at the plastic bag,
then again at the sculpture, shook his head, smiled, and walked on into
Laekjargata.

He pulled his hood up over his head and made towards the junction
of Austurstraeti and Laekjargata. He soon stopped walking, stood thinking for a short while in front of a large, brightly lit clothes shop, and
then crossed the road, to the spot where he had taken the taxi earlier
in the day. Once there he stopped in the middle of the pavement and
sat down by a square that was covered in paving stones and resembled
a gigantic chessboard. He took the wallet out of the bag and opened
it to find seven bills—eleven thousand kronur—and two photos: one
of a plump woman with dark hair and "Love, Mary" written on it in
English, and the other of an unusually pretty and well-dressed seven-
or eight-year-old girl, who was standing in front of dark red curtains
and holding an open book, probably the Bible, in her hands. When he
examined the wallet more closely he discovered an old driving license
in a tight pocket. There was a photograph of the pale man under the
cracked, matted plastic. He looked slightly healthier in the photo and
his hair was longer than it had been in the bar a few minutes earlier.
His name was Gisli Norholm, and that he was licensed to drive cars
and vehicles carrying passengers on a professional basis.

He pushed the bills and the photo of the girl into his anorak pocket,
replaced the photo of Mary and the driving license, stood up, and
dropped the wallet into the green trash can beside the chessboard. It
was still freezing cold, probably even colder than before. He was going
to sit down again but changed his mind and walked up the steps towards the restaurant at the top of the slope. Then he went up Bankastraeti in the direction of Laugavegur. When he reached the corner of
Klapparstigur and Laugavegur, he saw two policemen walking in the
opposite direction on the other side of the street. He disappeared into
an antique shop on the corner.

13

I had intended to wait for Armann—I was looking forward to seeing what he would buy in the duty-free store—but he was delayed once we entered the building and I didn't see him again until I had reached baggage reclaim. He was accompanied by an airport attendant. They disappeared up the escalator, as if they were going back out to the plane. Armann was in his heavy wool overcoat and was flapping his arms; the uniformed attendant nodded continuously. I imagined that Armann must have left something behind on the plane; whatever had happened, he had clearly had the sense to ask for help.

The blonde had disappeared too quickly for me to keep an eye on her and I didn't see her in the duty-free store either. I did however notice the educated woman with the hickey standing in front of the make-up counter; she was holding two pale green boxes of face cream and seemed to be trying to decide which one she should choose. I wondered if I should ask her to help me find something for Vigdis. I was sure that she had good taste, considering how she was dressed and the manner in which she had turned the pages of her magazine. I was just about to approach her when she put down both boxes and walked away. At that moment I decided to buy a good cognac and a box of chocolates for Vigdis.

The thought of Vigdis only made me think of one thing: the blonde from Hjalmholt. I looked for her in the crowd and came to the conclusion that she wasn't interested in hanging about with all the consumer crazy Icelanders; if anything she would have rushed through the usual selection, only taking a carton of cigarettes and a bottle of Campari or Russian, not American, vodka.

"We have to buy something for Eyvi," I heard someone say beside me as I stood in front of the cognac and whisky rack. The voice belonged to a man of about fifty with thinning hair. He was carrying an empty basket and reached up to the top shelf for a bottle of cognac.

"Why?" asked a woman of the same age, probably his wife, who stood on the other side of him. She sounded impatient.

"I can't be bothered seeing his pathetic smile if he doesn't get anything," the man said and gazed with a rather serious expression at the bottle, as if buying it was quite a responsibility.

"It's your decision," the woman said. "He isn't my brother."

It was obvious that the woman's lack of interest annoyed him. She had half-filled her basket with sweets. He put the cognac bottle back on the shelf and took hold of a cheaper brand in a plastic half-liter bottle. He examined it carefully, turned it over to read the information on the back, and tried the lid to make sure it was sealed properly. Then he said:

"He's been collecting our mail for the past three weeks, I think the least we can do is show our gratitude."

"I didn't ask him to do it," the woman answered just as coldly as before.

"No, I did," the man said determinedly. "I think it's quite alright to give him something for coming to pick us up and looking after the mail."

"He has been using our car for three weeks," the woman objected. "Isn't that payment enough for taking some letters and newspapers out of the mail box?"

I could see that she had said her last words on the matter.

"He's coming to pick us up," the man repeated, but got no response.

He still couldn't decide what to choose and I felt rather sorry for him. I decided to help the fellow; no doubt I was bolder than usual after the red wine and liqueur that I had on the plane. I apologized for interfering and told him that instead of the plastic bottle of cognac he should rather buy a big bottle of whisky or even port. The duty-free store had good port. The man gave me a look of surprise but I noticed that he was grateful for my advice. His wife, on the other hand, glared at me.

"That's an idea," he said, looking confidently at the cognac bottle. "Do you hear that, Magga?"

"I want no part in this," she said almost aggressively. "I don't see why we have to give your brother a bottle of alcohol every time we come home from abroad." Having said that she turned around and pushed her way through the crowd towards the make-up stand.

"I just can't bear to look at his pathetic smile," the man repeated almost whining, more to himself than to his wife who was no longer there to listen to him. He gave a nod in my direction to show he appreciated the advice. Then I showed him a liter bottle of malt whisky, imagining that this Eyvi would be happy with a bottle like that. By now, he would no doubt be standing with his face pressed up against the glass that separates the passengers, who have just landed, from those who have come to meet them.

"So this is good, you say?" the brother asked when he had put the cognac back and picked up the liter of malt whisky instead. He glanced nervously over his shoulder. As I nodded, I pulled my bottom lip over my top one and tried to give him the impression that he was being given advice by a specialist. I quite expected him to ask for more advice, perhaps chat a little now that his wife had gone off, but he was satisfied with what I had already told him, placed the bottle carefully in his basket, and added another liter of malt whisky. Then he thanked me again and went off, clearly pleased with his purchases.

I hadn't intended to buy whisky but while I imagined Eyvi and his brother in the living room with both bottles on the table—it wasn't easy to guess whose bottle had been opened—I put one in my basket. Then I chose a good cognac and some Belgian chocolates for Vigdis. I added a liter of dry martini and two cartons of Camel filters, as well as cigars that looked as though they were one hundred percent tobacco, though it wasn't stated on the box. Before placing everything on the counter, I grabbed six cans of beer too. I expected to be told that I had exceeded the allowance, but I wasn't stopped at the counter or at the customs gate.

I still hadn't seen the fair-haired woman, but I had spotted Armann again and it was obvious that he was having some trouble. I decided not to bother about him. Instead, now that I had gotten through customs, I cheered myself up with the thought that I was a free man and after four hours of going without could even enjoy a cigarette. I welcomed myself and pulled my overcoat out of my suitcase. It was cold in the entrance but I enjoyed the fresh air and looked forward to settling down on the bus.

First of all I had to have a smoke. While I was unwrapping the pack of Hamlets that I had bought at Heathrow, I looked across the hallway and amused myself by wondering if Eyvi had arrived to pick up the couple from the duty-free store. I was keeping an eye out for the blonde woman at the same time. I saw two men who could have been Eyvi. One of them was half bald and wore a dark blue fleece jumper and grey Terylene pants and the other, whom I recognized from somewhere downtown—either he worked in a shop or at the Post Office—was quite like the brother, with thinning fair hair, running shoes, and some kind of tracksuit under his anorak. He was holding a set of car keys that he rattled to announce his arrival.

When I walked outside, I saw the couple in front of me looking in the direction of the car park. The Fly Bus had arrived and the driver had started to load suitcases into the luggage compartment. The couple stood surrounded by their suitcases and duty-free bags and were looking rather miserable, not exactly dressed for February's frost. I lit a cigar and took a sip from the Cointreau bottle from the plane. When I looked at them again, the woman seemed to be quietly scolding the man—I imagined it was because of the whisky he had bought—and I didn't think she did much to warm him with her hard, fierce expression. I strained my ears to catch what she was saying and seemed to hear her mention the bus. A few minutes later the man walked slowly back towards the entrance of the airport building. He stopped close to me, turned around, and looked at his wife, as if he was tired rather than annoyed. Then he carried on and went inside.

The frost was beginning to sting my cheeks. I put out the half-smoked cigar and was about to get into the bus, but when I swung my bag up on to my shoulder I noticed the blonde woman standing outside the door with her luggage. She was lighting a cigarette. I had another drink from the miniature bottle and got out a pack of cigarettes from my coat pocket as I walked over to her.

"I have to ask you for a light," I said.

"It's alright to do it," she answered.

I was almost sure she was referring to what she had said when she came out of the toilet in the plane. The words were exactly the same, except instead of letting me know that it was alright "to enter," she now said it was all right "to do it."

14

It wasn't very bright inside the antique shop. What little light there was came from the weak yellow glow of lamps that were positioned amongst the dark wooden furniture; the atmosphere was better than the bar on Austurstraeti. He watched the policemen walk down Laugavegur until he couldn't see them any more, then he wandered round the shop and inspected the furniture and knickknacks. He stopped in a corner, sat down in a deep, wide armchair that was covered in dark green upholstery, and stayed there for a while. There weren't many customers in the shop: a middle-aged shop assistant stood beside a tall chest of drawers and arranged small statues around a mantelpiece clock; a young couple, who were holding a little girl by the hand, were interested in a beautiful sideboard with a mirror; and an old lady walked to and fro looking at different objects, fingered some of them but didn't seem to be looking for anything in particular. He stretched out his legs, slid further down in the chair, and leaned his head back. He held the plastic bag on his lap as if it was a cat and after a few moments he had closed his eyes and seemed to be asleep. It was warm in there.

When the old woman left the shop the doorbell rang, warning the customers to expect a cold gust of air. He opened his eyes and sat up straight in the armchair. The shop assistant had moved behind the counter; she was fiddling with a copper-colored standard lamp that had a light red shade. He got up from the chair, walked over to the counter, and said good morning. The woman smiled in a friendly manner and nodded. Carefully, he took the box, which contained the sailing ship, out of the plastic bag and, as he put it down on the table, said he would like to show her something. She asked what it was, and he turned the box round so that she could see the beautifully carved ship; her face lit up. He told her that it was from the middle of the nineteenth century and she replied that she could imagine that, without knowing anything about it of course. He put his hand under it and lifted it up so that she could see it better. When she asked where he had gotten hold of it he answered: "in England." He had bought it a few years ago in London for two thousand pounds. She nodded again and looked at him closely, as if she was trying to fathom why he was showing her the ship. If that was the case, the answer came immediately: was she interested in buying it from him, he would let her have it at a very reasonable price. She smiled and when he said that he would let her have the ship for a hundred and fifty thousand kronur, she laughed in a rather embarrassed manner. She wasn't so sure about that, they weren't buying much these days, but she was willing to let her husband have a look at it, he was the one who evaluated the goods here, she didn't have any say in such matters. Then he said that there was no doubt to be had about this object. If he let them have it for a hundred and fifty thousand he was almost giving it away. The woman said that she wasn't sure if there was a market for such objects. He interrupted her and said with a smile that he wasn't intending to sell the ship, he was going to give it to a good friend of his. He had only been curious to find out what he could get for it.

He burped. It seemed as if he had accidentally let the burp slip out; he put his hand in front of his mouth and mumbled a muffled apology into the palm of his hand. Suddenly there was a very clear change in the woman's manner. It appeared that something more serious than a burp had made the man seem highly suspicious. Her face showed how nervous she had become. The corner of her mouth twitched and she backed away. While he put the ship back inside the bag and thanked the woman, she glanced around the shop, like she was looking for the couple with the child. She seemed very relieved when he made his way to the door. He looked out of the window in both directions before stepping out into the street, then he took hold of the door and swung it slightly back and forth to make the bell ring. The shop assistant gave him a forced smile when he waved goodbye and left.

He walked up the main street and didn't stop until he reached a restaurant close to the bus station, Hlemmur. He glanced quickly at the menu in the window and then went inside. There were dark wood paneled cubicles on the left hand side that reminded one of an American country bar but many other details indicated that the place was run by Asians. To the right, near the wall, was a large dining-room table with a glass plate—it seemed to have been meticulously carved in an eastern fashion—and there were two short Asian girls standing at the counter. He walked up to them and asked, in English, if he could use the phone. They answered him in Icelandic: there was a pay phone further in, just before you come to the toilets. One of them gave him change for the phone while the other poured out the double vodka he had ordered as he asked for the telephone directory. He went over to the public telephone and searched in the directory. He dialed the number and waited but got no reply. Then he looked in the directory again for another number. While he flicked roughly through the pages he said the name Halldor out loud and repeated it several times under his breath, adding the surname Emilsson. He took a good sip out of the vodka glass and, just when he seemed to have found the number, he swallowed, which made him grimace and shudder. This time someone answered.

He asked if that was the number belonging to the parents of Emil S. Halldorsson and it obviously was because he stuck his thumb up in the air and moved his lips as if he was saying yes. Was this his mother then? He told her that he was an old school friend of Emil and that Emil had given him their number and had suggested he call them if he wasn't at home. Did she know if her son was in town? It was important that he contacted him, preferably today. He was abroad? Coming home today? Now, later on? He should land around five o'clock? Did she think there would be any delay? Most probably not. No doubt Emil had completely forgotten to tell him that he would be going abroad, he had spoken to him several weeks ago. He lived abroad himself and they weren't continually in contact. What, he went off when he won the lottery? He hadn't told him that either. He asked if he had won a fortune and smiled when Emil's mother answered. Good for him, going off; one didn't often get money like that.

He thanked Emil's mother and ended the conversation. *Later on.* He repeated the phrase to himself and replaced the receiver. He picked up his glass, tipped it up slowly to his lips, as if he hadn't quite decided whether he should drink it, and gulped down what was left without screwing up his face.

15

I wasn't particularly surprised to see the couple from the duty-free store get on the bus. I waited outside on the pavement with the blonde woman until the driver announced that he was ready to leave. We smoked another cigarette together and she told me that the customs officials had searched her. They had carried out quite a thorough examination, she said. To me, she didn't look the type that customs officials would have reason to pick on. She was wearing a neat black leather jacket on top of her T-shirt—she must have bought the jacket on this trip—and she had wrapped herself in a thick, black scarf.

I was just about to tell her that we had met before (though we didn't really meet), about fifteen years ago, but changed my mind. I would tell her later, if we ever got to know each other better, which I really hoped we would.

The driver had seen to all the baggage and had locked the luggage compartment. We put out our cigarettes and climbed into the bus. I didn't expect to see Armann in there—I hadn't noticed him come through customs—but I looked around for him before I sat down. He would obviously have to wait for the next bus; somehow I couldn't imagine that he would be picked up in a private car.

It seemed natural that we sit together, the blonde one and I; the only seats that were vacant were near the front of the bus.

"My name is Emil," I said when we had sat down. I thought it was about time I introduced myself.

"Greta," she replied, combing her hair back with her hands and tying it into a knot. "What were you doing in London?"

I told her that I had been shopping.

"For some company?"

While I explained to her what kind of shopping trip I had been on, I took two cans of beer out of my duty-free bag and offered her one. I was pleasantly surprised when she said yes.

"But what were you doing?" I asked.

"Smuggling dope," she said with a grin. "No, I was just visiting my sister who lives in London."

I hadn't noticed how beautiful her smile was and how full her lips were when she smiled at me on the plane. Despite the fact that fifteen years had passed, I thought her face seemed younger now, and I secretly tried to imagine her with ruffled hair, as she was when she emerged from the children's bedroom. There was something very sexy about her eyes, as if she was drowsy or, at least, not very wide awake, which, on the other hand, was a contradiction, because she seemed to me to be very smart and clearly had a sense of humor.

"Were you there for long?" I asked, just to say something.

"Yes and no," she answered. "I would have liked to stay longer but maybe not with my sister. I like being in London."

"But not at your sister's?"

"Yes, of course it's good to stay with one's sister in London. But I wouldn't have minded if she was sitting here now beside you instead of me."

I didn't quite know what to say to this.

"I didn't mean it like that," she said, as if she had read my thoughts. "I would just have liked to stay longer in her flat, that is without her being there as well. But, what did you say, were you just shopping? Not *doing* anything?"

"I was visiting a friend who is at university there," I said. "Just disrupting his studies, he's learning economics. But besides that, I was just wasting money. Or converting it into something else; one doesn't really waste money by buying something with it, of course it is still in circulation."

"It's still in circulation?"

"At least it doesn't disappear," I said, beginning to regret my stupid attempt to be clever. "I mean the money I took with me, it's in London now," I explained and tried to sound as if I was deliberately making a poor joke. "I didn't really waste it, I just exchanged it for something else."

"I see," Greta said with a good-natured smile.

"Well, I won the lottery a few weeks ago," I was quick to add, trying to steer the conversation away from this silly remark about wasting money. I realized straight away that I had made matters worse; it was stupidly naive to tell a complete stranger that one had won the lottery. But her reaction didn't seem to indicate that I had made a fool of myself:

"May I ask how much you won?" she asked keenly.

"A million."

"A million?"

"Yes, one million."

"Then what? You went and wasted the lot in London? I mean, did you *take it all with you* to London?"

We both laughed. I answered that I hadn't wasted it all, and we began to laugh again at the verb "waste," which is difficult to avoid using when talking about money; we had made a new version of the word game The Lady in Hamburg. While Greta told me about her un-successful shopping trip, as she called it—she had spent a whole day in town, from ten in the morning till seven in the evening and hadn't managed to buy a single thing for herself—I began to wonder if I had bought enough in London, if the trips to the music stores and book stores had been as productive as I had expected them to be, if one can use such professional terms in this context.

As I started thinking that, instead of meeting on the plane, we had bumped into each other in London, maybe walked into the same bar and one heard the other order a drink, Greta asked—not in the imagi-nary bar but beside me here in the bus—if I lived alone or with some-one. I was surprised that she asked me this—I thought that these kinds of questions came later on, after you got to know a person better—but I told her the truth: I had lived alone for a little while now but had a seven-year-old son who lived in Denmark with his mother and came to visit me in the summertime.

"I'm in a similar situation," she said. "I have a five-year-old daughter, and I live alone. Or almost, I live in the basement of my mother's house."

We carried on talking for the rest of the ride, and I think, consider-ing how we had only just met, we were quite frank about ourselves. I didn't mention that I had a girlfriend and thought it was very likely that she was keeping similar information to herself. It looked like the romantic comedy I had imagined outside the toilet on the plane might actually reach its happy conclusion. We agreed to meet in the evening, she would call me after she had had her supper, taken a bath and so on.

Of course Vigdis cast a large, dark shadow over the excitement and nervous fluttering that I felt inside, but it had to be like that; I wasn't going to stop now, I couldn't do it to myself nor to this interest-ing woman whom—however illogical it was—I continually imagined changing the sheets and scrubbing bathrooms in the hotel rooms in Akureyri where Vigdis worked. I wouldn't see Vigdis for several days and told myself that I had to wait and see what would evolve with Greta. I couldn't even be sure that anything would happen. It could be that whatever was meant to happen had already happened. If she called, it might just be to say thank you for our conversation on the bus; she had to spend time with her daughter this evening and maybe she would contact me later.

Her mother came to pick her up at Loftleidir Hotel. I had already declined the offer of a ride with them. I would take a taxi as I had to stop at a certain place on the way. Despite the fact that I was impatient to spend more time with this new girlfriend, it was too much of an insult to Vigdis to ride in Greta's mother's car. While I watched mother and daughter drive off, I suddenly felt that the clothes that Vigdis had asked me to buy in London were unbelievably drab. I thought that it would have been a real *waste* of money to have bought them.

I couldn't decide if I felt good or bad. When I sat in the taxi and told the driver to go to Grettisgata, I saw a dirty white Hyundai drive up to the couple from the duty-free store. I found it rather amusing that I, though I knew nothing about them, just the same, knew the name of the man who stepped out of the car. And he, this Eyvi, didn't know that I, a complete stranger who at this very moment was driving away in a taxi, was responsible for the fact that his brother was giving him a whole liter of fifteen-year-old malt whisky, instead of some cheap cognac in a plastic bottle.

Still, I thought he might get nothing at all.

16

Before he sat down in one of the booths, he fetched a cup of coffee. He made a point of asking for a large cup of coffee, in a mug if they had one, and ordered another double vodka. There was a newspaper folded on the table. Once he had moved several empty beer glasses and dirty dishes over to the next table, he opened the newspaper and began to read. They were playing old, Icelandic pop songs on the radio.

He skimmed through the newspaper, then he folded it again and used it to wipe the table, which was wet from the previous customers. He gazed into space for a few minutes, sipping his coffee and vodka now and then, always the vodka first, then the coffee. He took the book out of the plastic bag and placed it on the table, after first inspecting it to make sure it was perfectly dry and clean. He turned the pages slowly. He wasn't reading the text; he just seemed to enjoy looking at the old pages. Then he closed the book and gently stroked the back and front covers, as if he were wiping off a thick layer of dust and didn't want it to spread all over the table.

Next he put his hand in the pocket of his anorak and took out the money and the photo of the girl with the Bible he had acquired in Austurstraeti. Then he got his wallet out from his inner breast pocket and took out a slim pile of bills. When he had added the piles together, he found that he had forty seven thousand kronur. He straightened the bills, put them down on the table, and, finishing his vodka, pressed a glass down on top of them like a paperweight.

He glanced around, stretched his neck to see the two girls at the counter, and little by little began to act nervously, as if he was waiting for someone and was excited about it. He tapped the book with his index finger, gulped down the coffee, pressed the palm of his hand down on the empty vodka glass, and suddenly raised his hand, waving in the direction of the counter and calling hello until one of the barmaids noticed him. She asked if he wanted something; he beckoned her to come over to him. She didn't seem to understand his sign language at first, but then she came out from behind the bar and walked in the direction of the tables; she had a puzzled look on her face. He smiled kindly at her and asked for her name. She seemed surprised, looked away for a moment, and then asked what he wanted. He smiled at her again—as if he wanted to tell her it was all right, he was just asking out of curiosity—and then he pointed at his empty glass and told her to bring him a double whisky with ice, no more coffee, just a double whisky with ice. When she told him that they didn't usually serve at tables there, he took hold of her arm and pulled her closer. She didn't seem surprised, and he asked her in a whisper if she would come outside with him, maybe into an alleyway nearby; he would give her fifteen thousand kronur, just for coming with him for ten, fifteen minutes. Either she didn't understand what he was saying or didn't want to understand. She pulled her arm away and said something about him having to come to the bar, she didn't take any orders at the tables. But he seemed determined to get what he wanted, and he took hold of her arm again and repeated his offer: just the two of us somewhere nearby, just a few minutes for fifteen thousand kronur. He pointed at the pile of bills under the glass. Now she understood him; the girl loosened her arm by hitting him in the chest. She told him firmly, without broadcasting it all over the place, to leave. She used these words in the infinitive and when he didn't stand up she called to someone named Kristjan. It sounded as if this Kristjan was the owner of the restaurant, and it worked. He stood up from the table, knocked his glass over as he stretched for his money, snatched up his plastic bag, and pushed past the girl in the direction of the door.

Several customers had noticed that trouble was brewing—one of them had stood up to be ready for trouble—and the other barmaid started calling for Kristjan. The girl who had been offered the money seemed determined to stay calm, although she was clearly offended. She watched as he left the place, bumping into the corner of a table on the way and swearing coarsely, both in English and Icelandic. He went as far as the corner of Snorrabraut and Laugavegur before he stopped and put the money back in his wallet. Then he rushed across Snorrabraut, though the traffic lights were red, and slowed down as he approached the corner of Laugavegur and Baronsstigur.

17

The familiar sound that comes from loudspeakers when the needle touches the black vinyl adds to the good feeling I have that this little flat, on Grettisgata, is my home, and that now I am back safely after being away. Maybe I wasn't away very long, but it was long enough to look forward to coming home, which isn't strange when one has bought a collection of books, CDs, and videos and is dying to switch on the stereo in the living room. I get a wonderful shiver when the first tones of "Lonely Fire" pierce the heavy, two-week-old air, to which I have added the smoke from one of the Hamlets that I bought at Heathrow.

I wonder whether I should perhaps have invited Tomas up for a cup of coffee—he looked so cold out in the garden—but I decided against it. He must understand that I am not going to put myself out for someone, as my grandmother would have said, when I have just arrived home from abroad. I feel I need to spend some time alone in my flat—listen to a little music and even lie down on my bed—before I start entertaining others.

The living room window seems to be frozen shut when I try to open it. I don't dare to press hard on the single sheet of glass, so I decide to go out into the garden to see if I can scrape away the ice from the outside. While I'm putting on my shoes, I put my hand into my shirt pocket automatically—as I usually do before going outside, to make sure that I have some change or a credit card with me—and find something unexpected. Before I pull it out of my pocket, I realize what it is: Armann Valur's glasses.

"I don't believe it!" I say out loud to myself. It's exactly the last thing I need at the moment. I remember straight away that I put them into my shirt pocket when I passed the food tray to the flight attendant, but can't understand why on earth Armann didn't miss them when he woke up.

I try not to think of where Armann is at this moment. No doubt he has made them turn everything on the plane upside down. If his panic—flapping his arms in front of the airport official—was anything to go by, it didn't seem likely that he would leave the airport without his glasses. Besides, I know now, as I am holding on to the thick-lensed glasses, that he has considerable need of them. The only thing I can do is call him or try to contact someone at the airport; I am almost sure that Armann is still there.

I can't have been the one who decided to put the glasses in my pocket; someone else must have made the decision.

According to the telephone directory, Armann could almost be considered my neighbor; he lives on Raudararstigur. I am pretty sure I have the right man: Armann Valur Armannsson, Icelandic linguist. His phone rings four times before the answering machine clicks in. I must admit that I am quite surprised that he uses such technical devices, and I'm even more surprised when his message is repeated in English: "This is Armann Valur speaking. I am not in at the moment. Please leave your name and telephone number and I will see what I can do."

It's difficult to say if the last phrase is meant to be a joke or not and I hesitate for a moment before leaving a message:

"Hello Armann, this is Emil speaking, you probably remember me from the plane. I hope I haven't caused you too much inconvenience. I was just coming home a few minutes ago and I spotted that I've got your glasses. I am most terribly sorry, of course I didn't intend to . . ." I don't get any further: a shrill beep informs me that my time has run out. I immediately regret having hoped that "I haven't caused him too much inconvenience." Obviously the inconvenience that I caused him was "too much": I was responsible for him missing the Fly Bus into town and no doubt prevented him from buying some Opals in the duty-free store by depriving him of his sight. I had, at least, not *made his day*, although I realize that he probably isn't familiar with the expression. I can't imagine using the verb "to spot" will improve his opinion of me either. I call the answering machine again and ask Armann to contact me concerning the glasses, I'll be at home this evening. I rush to give him my telephone number before the beep cuts me off.

I put the heavy glasses down on the table in the living room and start unpacking my suitcases. I line up the wine on the right hand side of the table, place the cigarettes and cigars in front of the bottles, and pile up the books (all eight of them), the video cassettes (of which there are seven), and the CDs (there are thirty six of them, not counting those I bought for Saebjorn and Jaime) at the other end of the table. I have to laugh when I look at Armann's glasses in the center of the table, and I can't make up my mind whether this ridiculous mistake, this terrible misfortune, is worse for Armann or me. At least there is no special good fortune involved; I realize that we are about to meet again, the linguist and I.

I light a cigarette, open a warm beer from the duty-free pack, and go into the bedroom to have a look at my emails. Greta comes to mind. I wonder if I'll ever get to know her well enough to receive emails from her. At this moment she is probably telling her daughter about the double-decker buses in London and how the people drive on the wrong side of the road, but she won't mention the man she met on the plane on the way home and again on the bus, nor the fact that she intends to meet him this evening once the little one has fallen asleep.

There are about twenty emails waiting for me on the computer: several from Saebjorn and Jaime; one from Jonas, my friend in London, that was written today (no doubt asking, for the sake of politeness, if I've arrived home safely); two from Vigdis; a few from some magazines I subscribe to; and all sorts of junk mail.

I feel I need to cheer myself up and decide to make instant coffee with whisky. When I go into the kitchen and feel how heavy the air still is, I push the kitchen window open wider.

18

He was half way across Baronsstigur when he suddenly turned round and went back in the direction of Snorrabraut. He pulled down his hood and stood for a little while by a shop window, in front of a dummy which was dressed like a teenager. He looked at his reflection in the glass, ran his fingers through his thick hair, and spat into the palm of his hand, so that he could flatten his hair a bit on one side. Then he carried on at a quicker pace and went into a clothing shop; the mannequins in the window stood stark naked and were spotlighted in the cold darkness that now enveloped the city. He undid the zip on his anorak, walked straight up to the counter on the right, and asked a neat, dark haired man in his forties if he could keep his plastic bag while he had a look around. The man took the plastic bag without uttering a word and when the bag owner had turned his back to gaze around the spacious shop floor, the dark haired assistant went over to his colleague at one of the cash registers, pointed out the customer to him, and said something that made him smile. They watched him walk into a department on the left, come out again, and look at himself in the full-length mirror on the wall by the entrance, but when he came back in the direction of the counter they looked away and pretended to be busy with some imaginary tasks.

When he had made a complete circuit of the area beyond the counter, and gazed at and fingered several garments on hangers, the dark-haired sales assistant came up to him and asked if he could be of any help. He said possibly, he was looking for a suit, of rather thick material, a proper suit, as he put it, something he could wear on more occasions than just family gatherings. The sales assistant said he understood what he meant, he was talking about a suit he could wear both for funerals and on more relaxed, informal occasions, an everyday suit; he knew just what he meant. He stretched out towards a light grey one and told the man that if he himself was looking for a suit this is the one he would choose. It doesn't matter where you are, he said, this suit is always appropriate. He took the clothes, examined them from the front and the back, and then asked to see something else slightly darker, maybe even black, but it had to be darker. Let's look more in this direction then, the sales assistant said, and motioned him to follow.

Before he selected another suit he had a better look at the customer, mumbled something to himself about the size he needed, then showed him a charcoal-colored suit that seemed to fulfill his requirements about utility and thickness. The customer's reaction was positive; it was just what he was looking for, could he try it on? He was shown into the changing room and when he began to undress he shouted out to the assistant: could he find some fine shirt for him, something that would go well with the clothes? The assistant was standing in front of the changing room with a light grey shirt when he appeared in the suit, shoeless, and with his hands outstretched. You have to put on your shoes, the assistant said, it doesn't look right with just socks. Apart from that it fits like a glove, I think the size is just right, that is, if you want my opinion. He said he thought so too, took the shirt, put it on, and placed his feet into his shoes. The assistant showed him that he looked first class by forming a zero with his first finger and thumb and told him he would give him the shirt, this very fine shirt, made of the best quality material, for half price with the suit. He could also show him a tie that would go very well with the shirt. He said no thank you, he was not interested in ties or bow-ties, but perhaps he could dispose of the old clothes for him, everything except the anorak and shoes. The assistant said that was no problem, said he would fetch the clothes personally from the changing room later. Then he accepted payment, tapped a simple drum beat on the counter, and said that was fine, now they were quits.

On the way out, the customer paused by the full-length mirror and gazed at himself for a little while, pulling his anorak away from his shoulders to see more of his new suit, but he stopped as he was about to button up the shirt's top button and walked back to the counter. He had forgotten to take the plastic bag with him. The dark-haired man had disappeared from the counter, but the other assistant passed him the bag and told him with a smile that the outfit he had chosen was cool. The smile remained on the face of the assistant until he had left the shop. It was a cold smile, and he waved at the customer's back with his index finger, just like a child who hasn't gained control of all the movements of his body yet. He nearly fell when he stepped out on to the pavement. He swore automatically, stopped for a short while in front of the shop window, pulled up his hood, and zipped up his anorak.

After walking for a few minutes he disappeared into a store, where he asked if he could make a telephone call. While he was looking for the number in the directory, he said he wanted to buy cigarettes, one pack of Viceroy and something for his throat, something strong for his throat. Then he pressed the numbers. He waited for a short while and gazed absentmindedly into space, then he suddenly jerked into life, pressed the receiver closer to his ear, and slammed it back down. He said yes very decisively, like someone who has successfully completed a mission, and flicked his hands away when the shop assistant asked if he had said something. He paid for the cigarettes and throat lozenges, but corrected the man when he was going to charge for the phone call— the line was busy. Then he left and walked slowly up Vitastigur.

He stopped on the corner of Grettisgata, put his hand in his pocket for a cigarette, and lit it. He looked in both directions and pointed alternatively up and down the street, as if he was showing himself the way or asking which direction he should go. A big truck came up Vitastigur and braked suddenly at the corner of Grettisgata to allow a small white car to cross. It came speeding along from the west, obviously going much too fast for the road conditions. The truck driver watched the white car disappear, almost as if he was watching a ball spin over a tennis court. He had trouble with the ice when he tried to drive off. The wheels of the truck spun for a little while; then he let the truck slide backwards into a vacant parking space in front of the dry cleaner's on Vitastigur.

It was nearly six o'clock. A middle-aged man came running up the street from Laugavegur; he had a full plastic bag—a white bag that swung back and forth as he ran—in one hand. Then he suddenly stopped after passing the dry cleaner's, turned around, and disappeared into a doorway. He disappeared just like any other stranger: you don't expect to see them again in this life.

19

Cold, fresh air streams in through the wide open kitchen window. I begin to think spontaneously of Armann's speculations about the rise and fall of temperatures in the world; in a short while I'll be standing on the line between these great opposites (or however he expressed it): the cold coming in through the window and the water which I am going to boil for the coffee. I fill the smallest pot with icy cold water and switch on the burner. However, I don't know why I fill the pot for one little cup of coffee; I just feel uncomfortable watching such a small quantity of water boil. Probably, deep down, I am afraid that I will forget the pot on the burner, the water will evaporate, and the pot will burn and turn black inside.

The last sounds of "Lonely Fire" fade away. I turn the record over and turn the volume up slightly before I go back into the bedroom and answer the email from Vigdis. I'm aware that it is rather loud—the music itself isn't exactly very quiet—but I think it's all right to let Bella upstairs know that I am home. She will no doubt be very happy, if I am to believe what Tomas told me just now, that she couldn't find a better neighbor than me.

I seem to be surrounded by elderly people. I would think Bella is nearly eighty. Tomas next door could be about sixty-five, and an elderly couple and their middle-aged son live in the little house to the east.

Although there wasn't much truth in the newspaper ad for the flat—in particular the information regarding its size and condition—at least one detail was correct: it is in a quiet district.

Part
Two

The Pocket Money

1

I have just settled down to write an email to Vigdis when there is a knock on the front door. When I get up from the computer someone knocks again, twice as fast this time, and before I open the door I decide to peep out of the living room window to see who it is. While I open the curtains slightly, there is another knock, this time so insistently loud that I take extra care not to be seen as I peer out through the crack. When I see a man in a blue nylon anorak with a hood standing outside the door, I presume that this is the man who Tomas told me had come at lunchtime. My suspicions are confirmed when I see he is carrying a white plastic bag.

He continues to knock, not as often as before but even louder, and I risk putting my head a little closer to the window to see if I can get a glimpse of his face. The next moment he takes several steps backwards and looks up at the building, as if he expects me to be watching him from the floor above. I still can't see his face properly, because of the hood, but as I watch his movements—how he lifts his body and lets it slump down somehow with each step—it dawns on me.

I know who he is.

I automatically close the curtain and take several steps back from the window.

"Can it be?" I whisper to myself. "Can it really be?"

According to what I had heard, which was confirmed by his father several months ago, Havard Knutsson was kept in an institution in Sweden and should be in custody there for at least the next three years. He had only spent one year in this "so-called home," as his father Knutur referred to it.

"Can it really be him?" I wonder and refuse to believe it. I almost feel as if I have seen a ghost, and I begin to imagine that Havard died in the institution and his ghost has started knocking on people's doors—people who he knows wouldn't let him enter in the flesh. But the heavy blows on the door are too realistic to allow me to pretend that he's a ghost who would vanish when I opened the door. I try to convince myself that what I thought I saw in this man's movements was a mistake, I had only imagined the worst; this man outside may be someone completely different from the man he appears to be. But I don't manage to convince myself. There is only one person in the world who moves like this; it *is* Havard.

He grips the door knob again, then knocks several times and calls my name; he seems quite confident that I am at home. I immediately suspect that his next move will be to peep in through the mail slot, and before that can happen I decide to tiptoe across the floor, as silently as I can, and hide in the bathroom. Though it isn't likely that he can see me behind the thick curtains, I feel completely exposed in the living room. On the way to the bathroom I see steam rising from the pot on the stove; the water for the coffee has started to boil. If Havard peeped through the kitchen window at lunchtime, I think it's likely he'll do it again now. I don't hear anyone knocking, which must mean that he has gone or is standing outside the kitchen wondering how he can get in through the window. The music that I had just turned up—perhaps too high—doesn't sound as good now as it did earlier.

There is a knock on the glass and I don't have to wonder whether it is the kitchen or the living room window. If there is something that I am certain of at this moment, it is that Havard has noticed the pot on the stove and is standing outside the window calmly trying to decide whether he should do his old mate a favor and remove the pot from the stove or just leave it and go away. While I ask myself what I would do in his position, I can hear that he has come to the same conclusion as me; I hear the latch being lifted and know instinctively that he is forcing the window open. Without a second thought I rush from the bathroom to the bedroom. I realize that I am taking quite a risk and it is very likely that Havard has seen me; one can easily see the hall between the bathroom and the bedroom from the kitchen window. In order to see if he has come in, or if he even intends to come in, I peep as carefully as I can out of the doorway.

Now I see him properly for the first time; he has pushed down his hood and poked his head in through the open window. I notice that his hair is longer than when I saw him last, five years ago. He has a grip on the shelf above the sink and it is quite clear that he is going to heave his body through the open window. I don't dare to look any longer; any second now he could lift up his head and I probably wouldn't have time to draw back. Besides, it's not safe to stand in the doorway any longer. I try to avoid being in view from the kitchen window—except perhaps for one or two seconds—as I slide cautiously into the bedroom, stand for a few seconds in the middle of the room, and try to hear what he is doing out there. He groans as he struggles, and I imagine that he has gotten stuck on the window latch or torn a hole in his anorak or pants, when he suddenly says "damn it" and some other words that are drowned by the music in the living room.

I get down on my knees without even thinking, poke my head under the bed, and pull out a box of toys that belong to my son Halldor. I then lie down on the soft carpet, squeeze my body in under the bed, and pull the sheet down to the floor—to hide myself from the doorless entrance to the bedroom and from the window that faces the dim back garden.

I still find it difficult to believe that it is actually Havard in the kitchen, that the man would even dare to visit me at all. And why on earth does he have to choose today? I thought I had seen the last of Havard Knutsson; once again I have found out how ridiculous it is to believe something in this life.

I hear a noise through Big Fun's loud guitar playing, like something heavy falling on to the floor. There seem to be two thumps, then the window bangs shut; I think it is bound to break, but I don't hear the sound of broken glass.

There is no doubt about it, Havard is inside. He pants, and something that he notices—I can't imagine what—makes him exclaim with disapproval:

"What on earth is this?"

It sounds as though he is walking into the living room. I didn't see what kind of shoes he was wearing when I looked at him from the window, but they tap on the floorboards as he walks. If I know him at all, they are patent leather shoes with pointed toes; I can't imagine that the Icelandic winter would have any influence on the type of shoes that Havard Knutsson wears.

"What cement!" he says indignantly, and the next moment the music has been turned off. "No wonder my pal Emil can't bear to stay at home!"

I repeat his words to myself: What cement. No wonder I can't bear to stay at home.

Cement is, of course, one of the first words that come to mind in connection with Havard: cement in its literal meaning. I don't know what to think about this unexpected visit. And I don't know quite what to expect. I haven't heard from Havard for about five years, since we sat in the kitchen on Brooke Road in Stoke Newington and I gave him four hundred pounds to go away. Go away as far as possible, much further than just out of London, preferably to another country. And he said—with a grin fueled by the two or three pints of Special Brew he had drunk before lunch—that if I could give him four hundred more then he would never show his face again.

I should have given it to him. Though there isn't much one can be confident that Havard will do right, I believe that he would have kept that four hundred pound promise. At least he has kept his word about what would happen otherwise.

He goes back into the kitchen. I hear the sound of bubbling water die down; he must have taken the boiling water off the stove, and I presume that he has turned the gas off, though it's not quite certain. More likely, he has just taken the pot off the heat.

2

"Hello!" Havard shouts. "Hello, Emil?" He is in the living room. I hear him move the bottles on the table, then open one of them, probably the whisky. "Is anyone at home?" he calls out. I hear the seal tear and

the metallic sound when the cap is screwed off; I can hear it clearly because there is no real wall between the bedroom and the living room,
just a partition through which one can hear almost everything.

"Not bad," he says.

Now he is sniffing it. I wait for him to take a swig, to hear the splash
from the fifteen-year-old whisky when the bottle is tipped up, but I
don't hear anything like it; instead he slams the bottle down on the
table and the next moment his shoes echo on the hall floor.

"Are you there, Emil?" he says, as if he knows quite well that I am
hiding in here and am only waiting for the right moment to come out
and surprise him.

I lift the dark blue sheet up one or two centimeters, and my heart
nearly stops when I see Havard pause in the space between the bathroom and the bedroom. I can't see if he is looking in here, but I hear
him whistle something and imagine that he is trying to decide in which
direction he should go. Then he grows silent, goes into the toilet, and
stops in front of the sink, no doubt to look at himself in the mirror.

"He can't have gone far," Havard says to his reflection. "The millionaire Emil S. Halldorsson."

How on earth does he know about the lottery prize? Who has he
been talking to? Who told him about it? It has to be the reason for this
visit. Unless it is entirely a coincidence that he calls me a millionaire,
which is most unlikely.

"What's that?" he says, surprised, and the next moment I hear him
screwing the lid off something, probably my aftershave, and slap his
hand on his cheeks or neck. "Après-rasage," he says with a hard French
accent, and then in English, before he bangs the bottle down on the
table beside the sink.

I was right about his shoes. He is wearing the same kind of shoes he
wore five years ago: black patent leather shoes with pointed toes that
have clearly covered a lot of ground; perhaps these are the shoes he
bought in London just after we arrived there together. On the other
hand, his pants—dark grey Terylene pants that droop down a little
over his shoes when he opens his fly in front of the toilet bowl—seem
to be comparatively new. I haven't seen him in this kind of pant
before.

He starts whistling again as he urinates. I turn my head and push it down into the carpet with as much strength as I can muster.

The air under the bed is terrible. When I bought the flat I got someone to rub down the rough surface on the walls, and the resulting dust collected in the carpet, where I suspect most of it still is. It feels as if my head is getting stuffed full with dust, which isn't exactly what I need in these circumstances.

By lifting the sheet slightly higher I see that Havard is still wearing his anorak. It seems to be torn above the lower right-hand pocket, which might have happened when he climbed in through the kitchen window. When he pulls the anorak back—probably to prevent it from getting in the way of the stream of urine—I can see he is wearing a suit and a light grey shirt, which I must admit goes very well with the suit. My first thought is that he has been shopping in Reykjavik on credit and expects me—who, in his mind, is quite well off at the moment— to help him pay the bills. He stops whistling for a moment, farts, and sighs happily, and when he starts whistling again I think I recognize "Habanera" from *Carmen*.

It is obvious that he has consumed quite a lot of liquid. He zips up his fly and, without washing his hands, rushes out of the door by grab- bing on to the lintel and pulling himself out into the hall. I don't re- member these abrupt movements of his. He seems to be in a hurry and I begin to hope, feebly, that he will leave soon, perhaps snatch something to take with him and then disappear before I return from the shop or from wherever he has imagined that I have gone. But these hopes are short-lived; he stops suddenly in the hall and comes back into the bedroom—my guess is that something caught his eye as he was coming out of the bathroom. He walks straight up to the computer, which is in the corner by the headboard of the bed, just beside my legs.

He sits down at the table; the old wooden chair creaks and his nylon anorak crinkles. I lie dead still and don't dare to lift the sheet. Havard presses one key on the keyboard and then seems to stand up from the chair. He takes off his anorak, throws it on the bed, and sits down again.

"'Dear Vigdis,'" he reads out loud, and continues in a lower voice: "'Here I am back from London at last. How are you? Is the hotel busy?

You told me the other day that you would be attending some meeting today so I shall just write to you. It was a good trip. I visited Jonas, though he was busy studying for his exams. Then I went to some concerts at Vortex and Pizza Express . . .' Concerts at Pizza Express! That's the damn jazz place he was always trying to drag me along to! You are such a pussy, Emil!"

Of course, that's not quite true; I remember once trying to get him to come with me to a jazz concert in London, but that was at Pizza on the Park, not Pizza Express. He carries on reading:

"'As you can imagine I bought some music and a few books et cetera . . .'" At this point Havard stops reading the unfinished letter and asks himself who this Vigdis can be. Then he carries on reading quietly, snorts at something I have written and stops reading when he gets to the words "to settle my accounts." He repeats the words out loud with a question mark at the end. "What on earth does the man mean: 'To settle my accounts?'" adding, in a husky voice as if it came from the throat of some grumpy old man: "Emil and Vigdis. Who are you fucking these days, Emil?" Next he pretends to be a small child trying to read from a primer: "Emil likes fucking Vigdis. Vigdis always says yes when Emil wants to go to bed. She wants Emil to be happy and Emil is always happy because Vigdis is so good to Emil. But now little Emil is sad because he went away and there was no Vigdis there. Emil misses Vigdis very much. He has written her a letter."

How is it possible that I know this man? There is nothing in my life or character that leads to the conclusion that Havard and I should meet. My reaction to this soliloquy is to imagine that the directors of the institution in Sweden where he was kept saw no other solution than to get rid of him, even though he still had to serve two thirds of his confinement. I can quite understand their decision. However, it is unforgivable—if that is the case, which I don't really believe it is— that the directors did not inform me and others who know Havard, in good time, so that we could take some precautions before he arrived in Iceland.

Now he has suddenly lost interest in the letter to Vigdis. He stands up and leaves the room. I don't hear him take his anorak with him. And when I am sure that he has gone out, I stick my left hand out from under the bed and feel around until I touch the nylon. I let go of it straight away to avoid dragging it down on to the floor.

I hope that he will get going now, but then realize that he is obviously going to wait for me; he has come a long way, he clearly knows about the money I have won, and he is going to make me suffer for not taking him up on his offer in the kitchen at Brooke Road. He knew quite well at the time that I had those four hundred pounds—or rather eight hundred—and from his point of view I could have easily managed without them.

He has started on the whisky. I can hear him unscrew the lid and fetch a glass from the cupboard. He obviously takes his time choosing the right glass and starts whistling "Habanera" again. The glass rings. I guess that he selects one of my blue Iittala glasses. Then he pours so much into it that I have to accept the fact that he is not leaving any time soon. That uncomfortable fact is made more blatant when he opens a beer can—if it isn't out of his plastic bag then it is the fourth from my pack—and walks into the living room.

I hear him going through the CDs on the table and after a few minutes the first tones of "Mysterious Traveller" by Weather Report can be heard. Though I am far from being in the mood for jokes, I find it really amusing that he should pick this track—it is so very appropriate.

"What is this!" he exclaims in pleasure, and it's quite clear that on this occasion he is referring to the music. He gets a kick out of hearing something that is strange; he feels that he is more normal and has more freedom to follow his own whims.

He is obviously interested in the things that I brought home, I listen to him reading out the titles of the videos and piling up the CDs like a stock of cards. I shiver with anxiety at the thought of the scratches that this treatment will inflict.

"Where can this guy be?" he says. "One doesn't start heating water and then run straight out to a bar! No, Emil, one doesn't behave like that."

I really wish that I could answer him but I'm not thinking of coming out. I didn't come home to meet Havard Knutsson!

3

We had only known each other for about a month when we went off to London together. And it was by complete chance that Havard, whom I didn't really know at all, accompanied me. I had just started working in a hardware store when a friend of my father, a former professional footballer and joint-owner of a soap factory in England, invited me to stay in the flat he owned in London for six weeks and take care of some animals that lived there: a cat, a rabbit, a guinea pig, and an ancient iguana that had been given to him by a Mexican colleague from the world of football. His daughter lived in the house, which was situated in Stoke Newington in North London, but she was going away on a trip to Europe, so she needed someone to look after the flat and the animals. The daughter, Margret Osk—who was always called Osk—had spent several years in London learning to play the violin, and I had even seen her play with a string quintet a few years back in Reykjavik. I met her father Orn at a party my parents held several weeks before Havard and I left for London. My father insisted that I talk to Orn because we shared an interest in books on waterskiing, mountaineering, and exploring, however strange it may sound. We got on well, and when Orn found out that I wasn't doing anything special at the time his daughter would be away, he invited me to use his house. He even offered to pay me pocket money, as he called it— more as a joke I think—while I stayed there. He told me that I could take someone with me if I wanted to, he would pay for another person as well.

I didn't take long to think over that tempting offer, and I remember phoning Orn the following day to see if it was still open. In the beginning I intended to go alone, but Havard was very interested when I mentioned the trip to my workmates, not least because I had blurted out that I could take someone with me. In the short period that I had worked in the shop I had gotten to know Havard a little, and although we didn't have much in common, which I was quite happy about, I thought that he was interesting to talk to, especially about music and taste in music—a subject which, of course, one cannot discuss in any depth. Besides I was much more receptive to odd and even dubious characters at that time, and I can't deny that Havard aroused my curiosity in this respect.

I don't remember if I agreed straight away or if I took some time to think it over, but the outcome was that he accompanied me to London. Originally, he only intended to stay three weeks, but when a month had passed I saw no other option than to kick him out.

It became apparent that the Havard who shared the house with me in Stoke Newington was not the same interesting Havard whom I had got to know in the hardware store. And now, as he appears five years later, it seems obvious that the Havard who climbed in through my window a few minutes ago is the same Havard who lived with me on Brooke Road. And that really scares me. I don't know what to do; I was looking forward to coming home, listening to the music I had bought abroad, having a drink to unwind after the journey, and talking to my friends (who, I expect, were also looking forward to seeing me). Not to mention the fact that I am expecting a visit from a woman with whom I have already fallen in love.

I decide to give Havard half an hour—an hour at the most. I'm not going to lie here squashed under the bed longer than that; I already feel as if there are cement works going on in my head.

4

When the phone rings I try to remember where I put it down last. The telephone itself is on the kitchen table but, when the receiver is lying somewhere else, it is often difficult to hear where the sound is coming from, especially as the ringing comes from both parts. I hear Havard stand up, he seems to bump into the table—I shudder at the sounds that accompany his movements—and he finds the receiver after three rings.

"Hello," he says. "Yes, it is Emil's house. Yes, yes. No, he just popped out for a few minutes, I think he must have gone to the shop. Yes, that's right, he is back: I think he must have gone to buy milk or something for coffee. Who am I? My name is Havard." He is quiet for a little while, obviously listening to what the person on the other end of the line is saying, but then he continues: "I'll let him know, I'll tell him that you called. No, I'm not a school friend of his, I just worked with him once. All right, I'll let him know. Yes, yes, he came back about half an hour or an hour ago. He's bound to be back soon, I think it's quite likely. Yes, alright, I'll tell him."

Then he says goodbye and puts down the phone.

It's unbelievable how polite he can make himself sound over the phone. I think it is unlikely that it was Greta, she would not have asked if he was a friend from school; it was probably my mother. Havard confirms my guess straight away:

"Loving mum just checking to see if her little boy has come home."

I don't hear any sarcasm in the tone of his voice. He makes it sound—strange as it seems—as if he really thinks a mother should know her son's whereabouts.

Thanks at least for letting me know that it was my mother who called, I say to myself. And at the same time I wonder why the hell one ever wants to get to know other people, or let them take advantage of oneself. One feels sorry for some poor fellow who happens to work in the same place, invites him to come abroad, and pays his keep, and the only thing one gets in return is ingratitude, rudeness, and the experience of being trampled on—quite literally. The only thing that is lacking now, for me to really experience his physical presence, is for Havard to lie down on my bed—not to fall asleep, but to make the springs in this old, dilapidated divan sink down onto my back.

I suddenly realize very clearly the ridiculous position I am in and carry on thinking about the problems that one creates for oneself by getting to know various people. One shouldn't let others into one's life. I only have to think of Armann Valur to confirm my theory; instead of behaving as I intended to on the plane, I felt sorry for him and spoke to him (so he wouldn't be bored, I mean), and did him a favor by disposing of his food tray, and now I have his glasses, which I know will result in me never getting rid of him again.

I could be enjoying myself right now if everything was going according to plan, if this man was not here on the other side of the partition, this man who brings nothing but trouble and the threat of misfortune, this truly faulty specimen who climbed in through my window and is now enjoying the comfort of my living room. He has already spoiled my pleasure in the music I bought by playing it.

Involuntarily, I'm annoyed at my neighbor Tomas for telling me about the man who knocked on my door at lunchtime; I feel as though he is partly responsible for Havard's arrival—then and again now in late afternoon—as if he knew exactly when I was expected home. Could it be that Tomas had found out when I was meant to land and had told Havard? I even think that there was a strange expression on his face when he told me about the man. Of course, I don't know Tomas at all, my neighbor who is now sitting indoors looking forward to the supper his wife has started to cook, completely oblivious of the fact that I have condemned myself to some kind of house confinement—not just in the house, but under my very own bed.

Havard has turned off the music and I hear him unwrapping the carton of cigarettes that I bought in the duty-free store. He has been strangely quiet the past few minutes but the silence is broken by his swearing; he burned himself on a match.

He must have lit the cigarette, and I guess that he has had a good swig of whisky; he lets out a deep "ah," as one does sometimes when spirits burn one's throat.

"Hinrik!" he says suddenly, as if the name has just popped out of his throat unexpectedly.

I try to remember if I know a Hinrik and Havard answers my thoughts—in the loud voice he uses when he talks to himself—when he says:

"Hinrik, mon ami in Breidholt. Why don't I call him?"

I can't remember any Hinrik in Breidholt, but perhaps that's not surprising; I don't know any of Havard's acquaintances, except for one fellow, a skinny boy whose name was nothing like Hinrik, who worked with us in the hardware store. He had a shriveled arm and a thick mop of dark hair, which was obviously meant to hide his peculiarly big ears but didn't. Their friendship seemed to be built on the fact that Havard protected him from two older workers who plagued him; in return Havard was allowed to tease him a little when I was around.

His kindness towards the dark-haired boy caused me to turn a blind eye to Havard's obvious flaws, which I was quick to notice. However, there is no excuse for what I suspect is brewing in his mind right now. He is thinking of inviting someone over to my place.

"Hello, it's me, Havard, Hinrik's friend, you remember me." It sounds as though he has gone into the kitchen with the receiver. "Has he come home yet?" he continues. "Will you let me talk to him for a moment?" And then, before the phone gets put down, he adds: "Here, thanks for letting me use your toilet earlier, I don't think I would have made it back without pissing in the taxi."

For some reason I get really annoyed listening to the way Havard talks to this woman and I'm about to crawl out from under the bed, jump on him, and tear the receiver away. But of course I don't let myself. I don't know how I would get him out of the flat in a decent manner, not to mention the fact that, when it comes down to it, I am afraid of this man. What he did, the final incident that led to his being locked up in this institution or home in Sweden, still upsets me, and I have to admit that I don't have enough belief in medical science or mankind in general to imagine that it is possible to cure a man as crazy as Havard.

As far as I know, he was accused of beating up a young girl not long after he returned from his trip with me, and he was interrogated in connection with another assault, though he was never convicted for it. However, about a years and a half ago, when he had moved to Sweden, he was found guilty of assaulting a fifty-year-old woman in her home in Gothenburg. I don't know the details of the case or whether it was a case of rape or attempted rape, I only know that the less one has to do with Havard, the less likely one is to be drawn into some kind of trouble. Not that I am afraid he will lay his hands on me, but experience has shown me that hardly a day goes by without him managing to cause some sort of trouble.

On the day we left England we hadn't gotten any further than the airport here at home when Havard started accusing the waitress at the bar in the duty-free lounge of taking his pack of cigarettes while he was in the toilet. That resulted in them refusing to serve him any more drinks at the bar and he "was forced to open his own supply," as he put it. On top of that he bought another pack of cigarettes to make up for the pack that I had tried many times to tell him had been taken by young German tourists who had been sitting beside us at the bar.

"Hello, Rikki," he says when Hinrik picks up the phone. "Come home? Yes, of course I have come home. No, I know. But I'll have to tell you about it, we must meet. What? Yes, I dropped in today and you weren't there! You were at work! So you have a regular job? You've just come home, you say? And? Do you have a gig this evening? A new group? Oh, really? The same guys then? Your wife told me that you only play on weekends now. Really? This evening? Here, I'll be there. Eleven o'clock? So late? And where? Where is that? OK. Great. You know, something funny happened to me today. I was in this bar on Austurstraeti and there were some complete jerks who attacked me and were going to steal from me and what do you think I did? What? Leave? No, Hinrik, I don't run away when someone is about to punch me. I walked out with eleven thousand kronur in cash and left those gentlemen on the floor and one of them was eleven thousand poorer. What do you say? Stupid? No, Rikki, that is just part of taking care of oneself. I don't take nonsense from others, at the most I take money. But, listen, you don't happen to know some guy called, let me see, what's he called again, Gisli something . . ."

He walks briskly into the bedroom, grabs his anorak from the bed and thumps down in the chair in front of the computer.

"Oh, here, I just realized I don't have his driver's license, I let him keep it, poor fellow," he says, propping his feet up on the bed. The worn springs squeak: it's as if an elephant has flopped down on the edge of the bed.

"He was some kind of Nordic devil. Gisli something, Nor something. No doubt half-Norwegian. He was only half a man, that's for sure. What are you saying? Where am I? I'm at my old friend's place, Emil. You remember, the one I went to England with: Emil Halldorsson. He's rather a pussy, but a decent sort of a guy, I mean, he's alright. You should see all the music he's got here. You'd be sure to find something that you could listen to. Loads of weird things, there was some awful stuff on when I came in. I don't know where those sounds came from, probably Hell. But listen, why don't you drop by, I'm on Grettisgata, quite far up. Yes, why not? I was sure you would be at home earlier on, I thought you were just playing in the evenings and hung about at home in the daytime. Eh? No, no, I'm alone here, I don't know what has happened to Emil. I arrived a short while ago and he had water boiling on the stove so he can't have gone far. Yes, why not? Drop by this evening? Before you go to the gig? Isn't it a good idea to have a little drink first, eh?"

He tells Hinrik the number of the house and says goodbye in Swedish. Then he takes his feet off the bed, gives it a shove with one foot so that everything shakes and shudders, and hops up from the chair. I feel as if I am about to be flattened any minute—that he'll throw himself on to the bed and break it. But it doesn't happen; he goes out. It sounds as if he takes his anorak too and when I have listened out for what he is going to do next, thunderous tones suddenly bellow out of the loudspeakers; he has put some rock music on and clearly turned it up full blast. He is quick to turn it down. The music disappears for a moment and then comes back louder and he leaves it like that; he is playing Elvis Presley's "Hound Dog."

And he has called me a pussy. And has invited his friends from some outdated band in Breidholt here.

It's almost as if Havard knows that I am in the next room and is enjoying rubbing salt into the wounds he has inflicted on me—both now and in the past—when he starts singing along with Elvis:

You ain't never caught a rabbit and you ain't no friend of mine.

5

The pocket money that Orn, my father's friend, gave us for looking after the house and the animals should have been enough for Havard and me to live on, but we were much too extravagant during our first days in London; I, by buying CDs and books and Havard, by buying clothes, including the shoes that I thought I recognized, and a rather expensive, well-made ukulele. I wasn't with him when he wandered around Denmark Street and bought that Hawaiian guitar—I was most probably in Waterstone's flicking through books—but I was present on the only occasion that I remember when he tried to play the instrument. For some reason he thought it was highly appropriate to play the ukulele for the iguana. It was meant to be some kind of "Galapagos

atmosphere," as he called it, but the sound he produced was as sad as
the fate the Mexican iguana was to meet three weeks later.

Despite the fact that we quickly spent the allowance Orn had given
us, we were by no means in difficulties. Havard had brought his last
month's pay from the hardware store and I had a reasonable sum, which
I had intended to use to buy a car at home. Havard, however, managed
to spend all his money—and some of mine too—in his last week in
London. He discovered that one could walk into certain offices—that I
initially took for printing firms because *bookmakers* was printed on the
signs—and bet on horses and dogs, amongst other things. He managed
to persuade me to lend him two hundred pounds after some dogs ran
away with the last of his money. Two days later he asked me for four
hundred pounds, on top of the four hundred that I had given him to
ensure that he would disappear.

But money matters weren't the reason for my asking him—or rather
ordering him—to get out. Money is something that one can always
obtain again, even if it has disappeared once.

6

He doesn't seem to have the patience to listen to a short song like
"Hound Dog" right to the end. He switches off the stereo just as the
guitar solo begins and it sounds like he is going into the kitchen to
fetch more whisky. Then he takes several minutes choosing something
new to play. He whistles something out of tune and I—who have really nothing better to do—try to find out from his whistling what his
musical preferences are at the moment. I cross my fingers in the hope
that he will leave the turntable alone; I still haven't forgotten the terrible sound I heard when he scratched the needle across the shiny,
immaculate vinyl recording of Bizet's "Pearl Divers" that belonged to
Orn's daughter, Osk, on Brooke Road.

After several bars of "Computer World" by Kraftwerk, the phone
rings and Havard turns down the sound of the mysterious Germans
before answering.

"Emil's place," he says, as if he is acting as my secretary. "Emil? No,

he isn't . . . Armann? Armann Valur? Glasses? Did he call you? Just
now? Yes, he had to go out for a minute, I'm expecting him in a short
while. Yes, yes, we will be here. Just knock. What are you saying? Yes,
that's it. It stands back from the street, you'll see a garden with a white
fence, go into it and then you're there. In half an hour? A quarter of
an hour? The glasses? Wait a moment, I'll have a look."

I hear him move the CDs on the table and before I know it he is
standing in the hall by the bedroom door, no doubt trying to get away
from the music.

"Here, I've found some glasses, they have . . . yes, that's right. Quite
thick, yes. OK, just come along."

He hangs up, walks into the bathroom, and copies the sound of the
drums—or rather the drum machine—that is coming from the music
in the living room. I lift up the sheet a fraction. I can't see a cigarette
in his hand, but I detect the faint smell of tobacco smoke. He stands
there for a little while, and seems to be stretching his face towards the
mirror above the sink. For a few seconds he taps one of his feet on the
floor, though not in time to the music.

Although he has already been here twenty minutes or half an hour,
I still find it strange; I still can't believe it. I tell myself that I may be
having a nightmare. But just maybe. There is so little chance that it is
impossible. In other words, it is reality. It is reality with a capital R; the
most emphatic R I have ever experienced in reality.

What Havard does next makes the reality—at least the reality that
I experience from two and a half meters away—even more meaning-
ful, although I don't know whether there is any meaning in reality. By
lifting the sheet slightly higher, I see him take off his jacket, put down
the lighted cigarette on the edge of the sink, and begin to undo his
belt. Then he drops his pants to the floor, lifts his shirt and pulls down
his white underwear. I can't see his face—I would need to lift the sheet
dangerously high—but I get a full view of his penis in profile (if one
can talk about such things in profile); it's thick, though not very big,
and strangely dark, as if it had been sunbathing on its own. Havard lifts
it with the palm of his hand, pulls it out, and moves it up and down
until it begins to stiffen. My heart begins to beat faster. Now I feel like
I am prying into Havard's life, but I know that if I let the sheet fall

he is likely to notice. So I am sort of forced to watch. When his penis has started to stretch upwards, Havard suddenly stops playing with it. He lets his shirt fall down, turns his back to the door, and opens the toilet. Before he sits down on the seat I notice how white his legs are, especially compared to his dark penis.

While he is sitting I let the sheet fall down carefully to the carpet. Though I have the opportunity to see his face while he is sitting on the toilet, there is more chance that he will look into the bedroom from that position; besides, I have had enough of prying into his life, at least for the time being.

I can't help hearing the noises that accompany what he is doing. He takes his time, though he doesn't seem to be having any difficulty, and when I hear him stand up and flush the toilet, we are halfway through another track. Then, suddenly, I become aware of the smell from the toilet, and when it gets stronger—I could say disgustingly strong—I think of a sentence from *Herzog*: "Do you think I could give myself to a man whose shit smells like that!"

While Havard is calmly doing up his pants, I suddenly feel a tickle in my nose and realize that I'll have to sneeze sooner or later. I ask God to let Havard turn on the tap, or do something noisy, when I hear water start pouring forcefully into the sink; God seems to be listening to me. I bury my face in my hands and smother the sneeze as well as I possibly can. Then I wait in suspense for Havard to turn off the tap and search the bedroom, but nothing happens. The water keeps pouring into the sink and I begin to hear heavy sighs from Havard, sighs that soon change into rapid groans. I lift up the sheet one or two centimeters—enough to see up as far as Havard's waist—and watch him press his thighs against the sink. His right hand goes up and down; he is masturbating. Not only is he about to soil my sink but he drags Vigdis's name into it too; I think I can hear her name being called between groans. He wants her "to come here," he wants to show her something, she will have to bend down, and then, all at once, as if he wasn't quite expecting it, he comes; he lifts his body up and presses even harder against the sink. Compared to his previous groans, the sound he makes when he ejaculates is half choked, as if he is disappointed, as if Vigdis hasn't done what he had told her to do.

I try not to imagine how he will clean up or if he will bother to at all. I lay my cheek down on the carpet and shut my eyes; I feel like I have been straining to do something difficult too. The water continues pouring into the sink, and when it finally stops Havard goes into the living room and plays the first track of the CD again. Soon he starts singing—or rather talking—along to the music from the loudspeakers:

Interpol and Deutsche Bank. FBI and Scotland Yard.

Then I hear him pouring something into a glass and lighting a match. He is still muttering the lyrics to himself:

Business . . . numbers . . . money . . . people.

7

When I hear Havard giving a toast in Spanish—he is no doubt rewarding himself for his achievement in the bathroom—I recall our visit to a little Spanish bar in a narrow lane off Oxford Street. It was around the time when he bought his ukulele. I remember the visit particularly well because it was almost the only occasion on which Havard and I had a sensible talk. He told me about his mother and father, who didn't consider themselves capable of looking after him when he was small because of their drinking problem, and how he grew up more or less with his grandmother who lived next door. When he told me about it I felt that I was listening to a sensitive, sincere individual, and I imagine now that he must have felt unusually well that day and was perhaps genuinely grateful to be there with me in another country. I don't remember his exact words, but there in the bar he spoke about people at home not understanding him; sometimes he felt as if he lived in a different world from Icelanders in general, but in the same breath he mentioned how comfortable it was to be in England and speak a language which no one else could understand.

Except me of course.

I told him I understood what he meant, and while we laughed at the idea that he should perhaps speak English in Iceland—as there would be a chance of someone understanding him then—I thought he was cheerful and ready to make the best of our stay in London.

But then, exactly a day later, it seemed that Havard had gone off the rails emotionally and intellectually, and with each day that passed he seemed to move further and further away from the equilibrium that he had enjoyed that afternoon. It is probably ridiculous to talk about mental equilibrium in a person who has just arrived in a new country and spends a large amount of money on a musical instrument which he has never heard of before, but, considering his behavior during the rest of his stay, he seemed comparatively normal as we chatted in this friendly bar—even though that was the place where he decided to call himself Howard and to introduce me as Email from then on. Emil was far too Scandinavian a name for the British Isles.

It was also in this Spanish bar that Havard explained to two native bank clerks why we were in London. When he had finished telling me about his past, he took out his new instrument to have a look at it and handle it, and the men at the next table became very keen to find out what kind of guitar it was. One of them thought it was a toy guitar, and when Havard told him it was a ukulele, they admitted that they had never heard of anything called that. We were both rather chatty after the beer and the Spanish brandy that the bartender had recommended and were quite willing to talk to these city men. All Havard knew about the instrument he had been told by the man in the shop. It was a special guitar from Hawaii and originated in Portugal, and, when he mentioned that Elvis held a similar guitar on the cover of his album *Blue Hawaii*, the men remembered it and thought it was quite remark-able. Then they were curious to know where we came from, were we from Holland or Germany? Their interest didn't diminish when they heard that we came from Iceland, and they asked what we were doing in London, since we weren't just ordinary tourists, as Havard put it.

"We are taking care of some animals," he told them and they grew even more interested. He told them about the animals: the cat Ratty, which Orn thought looked like a rat when he got it as a kitten; Moby, the albino guinea pig, which was named in honor of the white whale in the owner's favorite book; Dick, the rabbit, which came into the house the day after Moby, so it seemed logical to call it that (even though it was a female); and last but not least, Ahab, the iguana, a nineteen-year-old lizard from prehistoric times—the oldest animal on earth and so on. It was named Ahab because of its expressive eyes, which Orn thought must be as deep as those of the captain of the ship *Pequod*; he assumed that it would have the same wisdom and experience.

Orn told us all of this in the half hour we spent with him on our arrival at Brooke Road. He also showed us the flat, taught us a bit about the implements in the house, and set limits on how far we could go in making ourselves at home. Then he went off to the airport to board a plane heading for South America, where he was going to spend the summer on business.

"You are some noble Icelanders," I think I remember one of the bank clerks saying, and though I realized that he was gently making fun of us, I didn't mind; in fact it was understandable. I would think it rather amusing if I met two foreigners in Reykjavik who had come here specifically to feed some cats, hamsters, or even budgies.

Before the Englishmen said goodbye they asked us what we were called. They weren't particularly surprised at Havard's new name—they seemed to think it was natural for Icelanders to have English names—but when they heard Havard say my name they were perplexed and asked if it really was Email. We managed to convince them that it was and were very pleased with ourselves after they had left the bar.

I felt good that evening and, when we got on the last seventy-three bus heading north towards Stoke Newington, I was looking forward to staying at Brooke Road. However, things were to change and I can recall beginning to have doubts straight away the next day when I woke up just before noon, a little tired after our drinking session the night before. Havard had by then consumed two or three Special Brews to wake up and told me very proudly that he had given Ratty some beer in his milk dish.

8

The fact that I had witnessed, or at least heard, Havard's acts, which could have been private if he had closed the door, made it even more impossible for me to come out from under the bed. Although Havard isn't the type of man who normally hides things or feels ashamed of his human needs, I can't—by suddenly appearing in the living room—admit that I have been watching him on the toilet and, even worse, that I have seen him masturbating. What makes it even more painful is the fact that he used Vigdis and called out her name to arouse himself. I haven't just been prying into his most intimate, private life; I have confirmed what he said about me to his friend in Breidholt: I am a "real pussy."

To put it bluntly, I have become the guilty party, if one can talk of guilt in connection with the events that have taken place here. Whatever crimes Havard has committed in the past—which one must admit are more than a few—his entrance into my flat (if one can use that term) is far from being a criminal act. Turning off a burner on the stove that belongs to an old friend who is obviously not at home is much more like a good deed.

There is a knock on the front door. The music in the living room has been changed once again; now one of the CDs from the bottom shelf is being played—a King Tubby CD that I bought in London five years ago. As far as I can hear, Havard is standing in the kitchen, pouring more beer into his glass. I can guess who is standing on the doorstep in the cold and know, at the same time, that it is pointless to ask God for help this time. Havard will invite Armann in and Armann will certainly accept. He knocks again before Havard goes to the door.

"Good evening," says the new host.

I can't hear what the visitor replies, but Havard invites him in, he is going to fetch the glasses. However, I hear Armann's voice when he goes into the living room. He shouts, even though the music isn't that loud:

"Emil hasn't come home?"

"No," Havard answers, and I can hear him moving something on the living room table. "Here, wait a moment," he adds and turns off the music. "Won't you wait a while and see if he comes back?"

"Well, I wonder if I should," Armann says, as if he has something important to do at home and has to think about it first.

"Have a seat," Havard says. "Can I offer you a beer or something?"

The front door closes; I hear Armann take off his shoes.

"A beer, you say?"

Although I can't say I am overjoyed that Armann is about to accept a drink in my living room, I am relieved that he knocked on the door and not the friend Havard invited. At the same time I know that this friend will come later, it's just a question of when he will turn up. The same applies to when Greta will call, or Vigdis, Saebjorn, or Jaime.

"What do you say, can I offer you a beer?" Havard says. "I'm pretty sure there's one left."

"He wouldn't have any red wine by any chance, would he?" Armann asks.

I close my eyes automatically and cross myself in my mind: not only is he going to have a drink, but he is going to pick and choose what it will be.

"I don't think so," Havard replies. "I don't think he bought anything in the duty-free store other than a few beers and, of course, some whisky and . . . what else did he buy? Martini. Yes, and then there is this fine bottle of cognac, Remy Martini no less."

"Rémy Martin," Armann corrects him, with such emphasis on the "r" sounds that Havard can't resist teasing him. It was something I didn't really expect him to notice.

"Oh, is that right!" he says, copying Armann's pronunciation without sounding too sarcastic. "So you would prefer cognac?"

"Yes, thanks, just one glass. But I mustn't stop too long. I'll just wait for him a little while, I really must thank him for taking care of my glasses."

I have to smile. Does he have any reason to hurry? Do I really deserve thanks for having ruined his homecoming?

"Here, I hadn't thought of it but maybe I should make some coffee." Havard suddenly begins to sound just like a homely housewife. "It's just a question of whether old Emil has any coffee."

"What did you say?" Armann asks, and Havard repeats that he is going to make some coffee to go with the cognac.

I don't hear Armann decline the offer of coffee and I try to make out what he is doing, but I can't hear him at all. Havard, on the other hand, has started looking for the coffee in the cupboards and, just when I remember that I had bought coffee before I went abroad, he finds it and tells Armann.

"Just help yourself to the cognac," he says, and, as far as I can make out from Armann's answer, he seems to have gone into the kitchen too.

"We have to use the proper glasses, don't you agree? I wonder if your friend has some special glasses for cognac?"

"I don't know, I only drink whisky myself," Havard says. I hear him turn on the tap and fill the coffee jug. "He must have something like that, our friend is a man of good taste."

The cork is pulled out of the Rémy Martin bottle.

"And you say he just popped out for a second?" Armann asks.

"He must have, he wasn't at home when I arrived. He can't have gone far, there was water boiling on the stove."

"And the front door was open?"

"Not quite, no. The door wasn't open, I had to climb through the window. I couldn't let the water boil over."

"That is strange," Armann says. I hear him pouring himself a glass and expect that they have found my cognac glasses, which I keep in the lower cupboard.

"How did you get to know each other?" Havard asks.

"We don't know each other very well. I just sat beside him on the plane on the way home from London today. Or he sat beside me."

"So you weren't traveling together then?"

"Well yes, we sat together on the plane. I beside him and he beside me."

"But when did he call you, did you say?"

"Just about um . . . what . . . maybe three quarters of an hour or an hour ago. Must have been as soon as he got home. He just left a message on my answering machine, I hadn't gotten home by then. Of course I thought that I had left my glasses on the plane, so I spent rather a long time at the airport."

Havard asks Armann if he wouldn't prefer to sit in the living room. They have to wait for the coffee; it will no doubt take a while.

"And what do you do?" he asks, without mincing his words, once they have sat down.

"You could say I work with linguistics," Armann answers.

I'm quite sure that he's more than willing to discuss the latter calmly over drinks, but it doesn't look like Havard is going to give him the opportunity to do so, at least not straight away.

"Hey, why don't we play some music? At least there is no shortage of music here at Señor Emilio's place."

I don't hear Armann reply and imagine that he prefers silence to anything his host is likely to play. There is silence for a minute until Armann asks:

"What's your name again? I haven't asked you, have I?"

Havard answers the question and then says cheerfully: "A little classical music? Shall we put a little classical music on the player, eh?"

Armann answers, but I can't make out what he says. Then he raises his voice and asks: "So you are called Havard? Isn't that what you said?"

"My name's Havard. Havard Knutsson."

"Oh, yes? Knutsson? That's not a bad name."

I can remember that Armann had given my name a similar appraisal. Havard seems to be engrossed in selecting music or putting it on. I don't hear him until he suddenly offers Armann a cigar—from the boxes I bought in the duty-free store I'm sure. I wonder whether Armann will offer his new friend an Opal and then realize that he probably finished the box he had on the plane; he didn't get to the duty-free store to buy more because of the trouble over his glasses.

He declines the offer of a cigar, says he stopped smoking a long time ago.

The coffee-maker makes itself heard and I swear to myself in frustration at not being able to share their pleasure. When the music starts—some classical piece that I don't recognize straight away—I hear Havard go into the kitchen and call out on the way:

"Here, isn't that Mozart? I just put on some Deutsche Grammophon CD. Isn't it old Mozart?"

"No, my friend," Armann answers. He raises his voice so that Havard can hear him from the kitchen. "That is not Mozart." Maybe he read the cover of the CD, but he seems to have some knowledge of music, contrary to what I had imagined on the plane. "It's Mahler. A rather remarkable work, it's sixteen-year-old Mahler. Just about the only chamber work of his that has been preserved."

"Jawohl," I hear Havard say, mainly to himself. "Chamber music, yes." Then he is suddenly standing in the hallway. "More cognac?" he offers, and again I am amazed at how polite and cultured he can appear to be and how he manages to hide all traces of his character underneath the surface.

"Let it come, let it come," Armann barks, as if he is beginning to feel the effects of the alcohol and is ready for anything.

I feel a new wave of hopelessness sweep over me and ask myself again what I have done to deserve this. The first answer that occurs to me is that I am paying for the unexpected good fortune of winning a million in the lottery and for deciding to waste at least a quarter of it on a trip abroad—on music, books and videos—instead of using it on something that could be considered constructive, something material, something that doesn't just go into one's head and end there.

Someone turns down the heavy, emotional music—I remember now, with Armann's help, that it is Mahler's piano quartet—and I hear that Havard has come back into the living room when he says:

"Haven't we got quite a chamber atmosphere here now? It's a pity old Emil isn't here, he would be sure to enjoy it."

"It's not bad," Armann answers. "Not bad at all."

"But wait a minute, I'd like to show you something," Havard interrupts, and I hear him lift up the plastic bag. "I'm going to show you something special, something I'm going to give my friend Emil."

The crinkling of plastic gets louder. Armann makes a sound that usually accompanies pain or suffering, but I realize it is caused by the cognac that I bought for Vigdis.

9

"And what have you got there?" Armann asks, full of curiosity.

"This is a whaler," Havard says proudly.

It takes me several seconds to realize what Havard is showing him. He has the beautifully carved model of the whaler *Essex*—the ship that was sunk in the early nineteenth century by the mythical giant whale which Melville later used as his model for *Moby-Dick*. The carved ship belonged to Orn, my father's friend on Brooke Road, until Havard stole it and an original edition of *Moby-Dick* from 1851.

"A whaler, eh?" I can hear that Armann hasn't quite followed. "You are trying to say that you have a whaler in the bag?"

"Well it's not a speedboat," Havard answers, as if he thinks that Armann is trying to dispute the matter.

"No, it's not a speedboat, you're right about that."

"And it's not a submarine," Havard says with a laugh.

"No, no, it's a whaler," Armann answers. "I can see that now, it's a whaler."

Havard's theft of these irreplaceable objects made the last three weeks that I spent at Brooke Road after his departure completely unbearable. I had thought about making up some story about a burglary, but I decided against it at the last moment and told Osk the truth when she returned from her trip. Later on, I told Orn over the phone that my friend—the same person who had been responsible for the deaths of the iguana and the rodents—had vanished one day, without me being able to do anything about it, and had taken the valuables with him. Osk didn't take the news particularly well, as was to be expected, but Orn's reaction, when I called him in San José in Costa Rica, was one of surprise rather than anger. I couldn't believe how well he took the news. He didn't insist in any way that I find my friend; instead he advised me to stay clear of this Havard for as long as I could. The less we knew about this unfortunate character the better. He refused to consider my proposal of pro forma compensation for the objects, and when we met again two years later at my father's house he offered me the use of his flat whenever I felt like it; his daughter no longer lived there and he only used it now and again. What I appreciated most of all in Orn's generosity was the fact that he asked me not to mention the incident to my father; he said that we should forget about it, and so should Osk of course.

I understand from what I have just heard that Havard has come to give me the ship, and I begin to wonder whether the book might be buried in the plastic bag too. All at once I feel it is worthwhile huddling here under the bed—it's as if this pathetic confinement has suddenly acquired a purpose. But on the other hand, I can't be sure that Havard will leave the ship behind if I don't make an appearance; I am quite certain that he wants to hand over the precious object to me in person.

"Some woman, to whom I spoke today in an antique shop, was going to give me two hundred and fifty thousand kronur for it," Havard says. "Isn't it right to say *antique shop*? Or what do you think? It's an *antique shop*, isn't it?"

"I thought you were going to give it to Emil," Armann answers. He doesn't seem very interested in either the ship or the term *antique shop*.

"That is just what I am going to do. You don't really think I would give it away for two hundred and fifty thousand, do you? Oh, no, sir, that ship is not for sale. I borrowed it from Emil's relative while I was in England a few years ago and now I have come to return it. I have this book too: *Moby-Dick*, the original edition. 1851."

The plastic bag is crinkled again, and despite my joy that the book should also come with the ship, I think it is almost unforgivable that he dragged it around in a plastic bag—I can just imagine how worn and tattered the bag is.

"Now that is something!" Armann says and asks to see the book.

"You must be careful with it," Havard warns him. I find it difficult not to laugh. This advice, which actually sounds like it is meant for a child, is quite appropriate when one remembers how roughly Armann treated his paperback on the plane earlier today. I think about the woman who sat on the other side of Armann; how she turned the pages of the magazine as if it was something of extreme value.

"And you are going to give it to Emil as well?" Armann asks. He seems to be surprised, or even amazed. "The original edition of *Moby-Dick*?"

"I'm just returning it," Havard corrects him. "I borrowed it from one of his relatives and just thought it was time to return it. I have had it for at least five years now."

"Maybe five years isn't a very long time for such an old book," Armann says and laughs.

"Maybe not for such a book," Havard answers, "but it is for me. At least *these* five years have passed rather slowly for me."

If I'm not mistaken, there is remorse, or a touch of remorse, in his voice.

"But at least you have had time to read it, I presume," Armann says cheerfully, and I imagine that he is handling the book.

"Me?" Havard says in a tone that makes it clear that he is not the kind of man to read such a book. "Armann, why don't we put something more cheerful on the hi-fi?"

I was truly amazed at how long Havard had tolerated listening to the Deutsche Grammophon CD, but on the other hand I was looking forward to listening to the works of Alban Berg, which is also on the CD. That type of music would certainly not be very acceptable to his sensitive ears. A series of short pieces for cello and piano by Anton Webern is playing now, and I am sure Armann is enjoying them. So he answers Havard first by saying that he may change the music, he isn't going to interfere, but he adds that he thinks it is a particularly beautiful work which he hasn't heard for a long time.

"But you like Elvis, don't you?" Havard asks. He seems determined to liven up the conversation and the music.

"I can't really say I do," Armann answers, obviously still engrossed in the book.

"We'll just have it on low," Havard says and cuts off Anton Webern. It's clear that he has the Elvis CD nearby, as only a few seconds pass before the first track begins. It is "Heartbreak Hotel." Havard does as he promised; he turns the volume down but then suddenly adds:

"Here, I am going to play 'Hound Dog,' you know that song, don't you?"

Armann doesn't bother to answer, and I can't help thinking that Havard's interest in the song about the hunting dog must have been sparked by his remembering the premature death of the rodents, Moby and Dick. He stops "Heartbreak Hotel" and I have already started to hum "Hound Dog" in my mind. The volume is turned up as soon as the song begins and Armann says something. I can't make it out, but it sounds as though he isn't particularly pleased and feels that things could be better right now.

10

One aspect of Havard's character I got to know while we stayed on Brooke Road was his fear of the dark. I quickly noticed how uncomfortable he felt when he was alone after dark, and I got him to admit this weakness one evening, when he told me for the second time that he always thought he could hear someone behind him whenever he went upstairs. During the day he was often noisy, especially when he had been drinking—which was usually the case—but in the evening he was calmer and yet sometimes slightly apprehensive as he walked around the flat. I teased him by saying that he had read too many English ghost stories, but he gave me the impression that there was something else—something more profound—that was bothering him. I thought there had maybe been some incident in his childhood, which I had begun to imagine as rather bleak and joyless; I could just see Havard as a child, bent and hollow chested, surrounded by his grandmother's old furniture and belongings while his mother and father were drinking next door.

Havard wasn't very fond of the cat on Brooke Road, especially after it jumped on him on the sofa one evening while we were watching television. He was so startled that he dropped a glowing cigarette between his legs—it made an ugly mark on the sofa—and knocked over a mug full of beer which he'd placed on the floor. But he liked the other animals, especially Dick the rabbit and Moby the white guinea pig, and their acquaintance ended in a rather sad way. However, he never ceased to grumble about the names Orn had given them, saying that he couldn't see the humor in giving an innocent guinea pig a whale's name. Besides, Dick was by far the most ridiculous name he had ever heard for a female rabbit. He made no complaints about the cat's name though and no doubt thought it was appropriate.

I was on my way home from the supermarket when the accident involving Moby and Dick occurred. We had visited one of the local pubs at lunchtime—our favorite, on the main street of the area, its walls were lined with books—and Havard had gone home before me, he couldn't be bothered to help buy something for supper. In view of what was happening while I was in the shop, it was rather unfortunate that I bought guinea pig food—a bag of dry food enriched with vitamins—on that occasion.

I had given Havard the key to the house and had to ring the door-bell several times before he answered. When he finally heard the bell, he came running to the door and, with a look of despair in his eyes, pushed me towards the back garden. I remember being quite sure that he had broken the flower pot, which he had just missed so often while playing basketball in the garden. I always had the feeling that he made the guinea pig and rabbit nervous by bouncing that ball around. But on this occasion it was they—that is Moby and Dick—who made life more miserable (strange though it may seem) for Havard. When I reached the back garden, still holding on to the shopping bags, I saw them lying on the dirty, wet paving stones as if they were frozen; they looked all grey and exceedingly pathetic.

I remember Havard crouching down in front of the animals and groaning, "I don't know how it happened," but, by putting two and two together, I could see just as well as he could what had happened. I thought that the bag of cement, which Orn admitted he should have gotten rid of long ago, had been closed, and, when I asked Havard if he had opened it, he said no and claimed that either Moby or Dick had opened it. Still, one way or another they had both climbed inside the bag and were nosing about inquisitively in the grey cement when Havard came home and looked out of the window. He said that he had run out into the garden like a shot and grabbed the animals out of the bag. At first he had tried to brush the cement off them, but when he saw that that didn't clean their fur properly, he had pulled out the hose that was lying curled up in the corner by the kitchen door and turned on the tap. He said he hadn't had any doubts, as he hosed down the animals, that he was doing the right thing. He had tried to reduce the force of the water by narrowing the opening with his thumb, spreading the water over a wider area. When he put the hose down and bent to look at the animals, it didn't take him long—maybe two or three minutes—to realize that things weren't quite as they should have been. Not that it was a new experience for Havard; his life had probably never been as it was meant to be.

He said he had not timed it, naturally, but he guessed that the cement had only taken about four or five minutes to harden around the soft fur of the poor animals. It was, however, more difficult to say precisely when they had stopped breathing. I remember the first thought that came into my mind was that they had been walled up alive like the Canterville ghost. Of course there was no denying that the accident was tragicomic, and now, looking back on it—with Havard here, in person, in my living room, treating Armann Valur to my purchases from the duty-free store—I thought for the second time today that what doesn't kill a man makes him stronger.

These words are no doubt appropriate in certain circumstances, but it would be necessary to rearrange them so that they make sense in this case.

When we sat down to accept what had happened and take stock of the situation, Havard suggested that we buy replacements. It must be possible to find another albino guinea pig and another light brown rabbit in a city as large as London, and it wasn't entirely certain that Osk and Orn would ever see the difference. For some reason I found the idea rather distasteful. It was horrible to think of Osk coming home and noticing that the rabbit and guinea pig in the garden were not the same animals she had left when she went off on holiday. And Havard and I would pretend that nothing had changed. "Is that Moby?" Osk would ask, really perplexed, and we would coolly say that it was, as if we were rather surprised that she should ask such a question. "But Moby had a tear in its ear," she was likely to say next, and we would look as if we didn't understand what she was talking about; the ear had probably healed while she was in Europe. She had been away for a rather long time. Then she would look puzzled and think that Dick was a slightly darker color than she remembered and the guinea pig looked thinner; hadn't we given it enough to eat? After discussing these strange changes in the animals—which we naturally weren't aware of—we would sit down and have some tea or coffee and Osk's suspicions would remain unsolved, something beyond our human understanding, perhaps supernatural.

But, of course, I had the task of explaining what had happened when Osk came home about four weeks later. Havard had been gone for a while by then, and he had added to my worries by causing another accident (if it could be called an accident). What I considered even more serious was the fact that he had taken the whale boat and the book. What he did to Moby and Dick could have happened to anyone—or almost anyone—and I decided to tell Osk, and later Orn, the truth about the accident. Havard had only meant to help the unfortunate animals, no doubt I would have reacted in just the same way and grabbed hold of the hose. But it was certainly a more unpleasant ordeal having to relate the fate that befell Ahab. The story of the rodents seemed trivial in comparison; at least these types of animals are easier to replace.

I pause for a moment over the word *supernatural.* Here I am lying under my own bed, recalling the ridiculous death of several animals which my companion and I were paid to look after five years ago, and now this Havard, whom I thought had cleared out of my life and was under careful supervision in an institution abroad, is back to haunt me, standing just a partition's width away in the living room. Am I imagining all this? Am I all right? Is something strange going on in my brain, just as I imagined a few hours ago was the case with Armann Valur? Am I experiencing what I felt earlier today, that I don't really belong here, that this isn't my own home?

Is the eccentric up there playing with me?

All I need to do is shake my head to get rid of these speculations. Not even that, because as soon as the phone starts ringing in the next room they disappear.

"This phone won't leave us in peace!" Havard barks. "It's all going to end in a mess!"

That is just what I'm beginning to be afraid of too.

11

I have no difficulty hearing what Havard says on the phone. Before answering, he turns down the Elvis in the living room; he is standing with the receiver no more than a meter away from the bed. I thought he was going to come into the bedroom or the bathroom, but he stopped in the hall; I can see his shoes from where I am lying.

"No, he just isn't at home, not at this moment but I'm expecting him to turn up any minute now. Greta? Your name is Greta. I'll do that."

I hadn't expected her to call so soon. My watch is in the living room, so I don't know exactly what the time is, but, since I came home in the taxi at six o'clock, I can't imagine that it is later than seven-thirty or eight.

"Yes," Havard carries on, "I am . . . at least we are old mates. Do I know where? No, I'm not sure, he has just come home from abroad and he must have nipped out. He wasn't here when I arrived. It was open. Oh, really? So he hasn't come to you? This evening? You were going to meet him this evening? You aren't Vigdis? No, of course not. What? Vigdis? No, I just thought that . . . No, you're called Greta, you told me just now. I'm Havard."

The damn fool. I can't tell if he is mentioning Vigdis just for malicious pleasure, but I'm quite sure he thinks it is strange and probably thrilling that I seem to be involved with two women.

"Alright, I'll just have to tell him you called. You're coming over then? What? When you have put her to bed? Alright, fine. He will surely be back by then, Emil is not the sort of person to just go off. Alright, OK you do that."

Then he says "bye, bye" in an exaggerated feminine manner and I imagine—at least I sincerely hope—that Greta has put down the phone. Not because she might think that the person who answered the phone is gay—I wouldn't mind that kind of misunderstanding—but because his greeting sounded more like an insult. Only Havard could think of talking to a total stranger like that.

As much as I look forward to Greta's visit, the last thing I want is for her to see my place for the first time in this impossible situation. It was clear that she intended to come over once her daughter has fallen asleep—she would hardly be putting her mother to bed—and that could mean that she will be here within an hour.

"Here, you have to have another drink," Havard shouts from the kitchen, where he must have put down the phone.

"Trinken und trinken?" Armann replies, and it is even more obvious now than it was a short while ago that he appreciates my indirect hospitality. Besides, the alcohol has started to affect his speech.

"You are drinking cognac, aren't you?" Havard says from the kitchen, where he is still pottering about.

"There's still some left," Armann says with a laugh and adds in a rather loud voice: "Here, I must tell you something the bartender told me at my hotel in London."

"Yes, you and Emil were in London together, weren't you?"

"Well, we flew home together. But the bartender in the Cumberland Hotel where I stayed told me an interesting story. He told me why he became . . . well, almost exactly why he decided to become a drinker."

"Almost exactly?" Havard has come back from the kitchen. Just as Armann is about to carry on with his story, the phone rings again. Havard sighs and repeats that this phone just won't leave them in peace.

"It could be Emil," Armann says.

But I am not the person who answers when Havard introduces himself.

"Good evening," he says formally. "This is Howard Knutsson speaking. Emil? No, Emil just isn't available. And who are you, if I may ask? Who am I? Well, I asked first."

Armann obviously can't control himself and laughs, or rather giggles at Havard's sense of humor.

"What? Haeme? I think you have to repeat that! Emil's friend? What? Haeme?"

It is Jaime, my friend from Chile.

"What? When? I really don't know. I came to visit Emil and . . . Who am I? Havard, Havard Knutsson. Yes, he has come home. Yes, he came home but he went off again. Yes, you will just have to come around here, I should think that he will come back. Yes, yes, I'll be here. Alright, OK. Haeme, wasn't it? OK, sir. I'll let him know."

"Who on earth was that?" Armann asks after Havard has hung up the phone and cursed Jaime under his breath.

"Some friend of our host," he says without interest. "Someone called Jaime. I don't know where he was ringing from. I wouldn't be surprised if he was phoning from outer space."

It is obvious that Havard was only pretending to be unable to pronounce Jaime's name while he was on the phone because now he says it almost exactly like Jaime himself.

Armann clearly recognizes the name.

"James? Can it be that some fellow called James is on the way over?"

"It was Jaime. It looks like we will have to entertain more visitors," Havard answers wearily. It is possible that he is genuinely tired.

"I can tell you that Jaime is the Spanish version of the English name James," Armann continues.

"Oh, is it?"

"And he was a friend of Emil's? I don't suppose he mentioned where he came from?"

"From outer space," Havard says, and now his voice has a trace of annoyance as well as tiredness in it. "At least it sounded like that."

"The extraterrestrial James?" Armann seems to be getting more and more boisterous. He laughs and asks which planet the man came from.

When no reply comes from Havard—who seems to be in the kitchen, I think I heard the fridge being opened—Armann shouts from the living room:

"Well, I was going to tell you about the bartender at the Cumberland!"

There is still no reaction from Havard. It sounds like Armann goes into the kitchen.

"He was called Nicholas Blair. Yes, I remember it now, it was Nicholas."

"Haven't we heard enough about English jerks for the time being?" Havard snarls, though it clearly has no effect on Armann's storytelling.

"Some people are peculiar, it's as if they decide one fine day that they are going to be drinkers, though it is normally difficult for people to make decisions. But this fellow Nicholas received rather unusual encouragement to take to the bottle. It happened like this . . ."

At this point I lose the thread of Armann's story; there is a loud noise when Havard knocks a bag of ice cubes against the kitchen table—at least I think that's what he's doing—and then he starts crushing the ice.

"Then he poured water into the three glasses and . . ."

"Do you want ice in your cognac?" Havard interrupts.

"Not in cognac, Havard," Armann answers in a reproachful tone and then carries on: "Once he has poured water into all the glasses he picks up a little container—probably a little test tube from a laboratory—and from it he pours alcohol into one glass of water. Then he picks up another test tube and tells his pupils that it contains nicotine."

"Nicotine in a glass?" Havard asks in disbelief.

"Yes, nicotine in liquid form, just as you can have morphine or whatever it is called, hashish oil."

"Hashish oil?" It sounds as though Havard is becoming slightly interested in the story now that Armann has mentioned hashish.

"Yes, or whatever it is called. At least he pours nicotine into the second glass and makes it clear that there is just pure water in the third glass, though we don't expect them to have had much pure water in England, especially not at that time."

"At that time? What time was that?" Havard asks.

"It was probably in the fifties, he was no spring chicken, this fellow Nicholas."

"This Nicholas, your friend, was a pupil in this class, then?"

"Yes."

"And now he is a bartender in this hotel?"

"I have already told you that, yes." Armann says, sounding annoyed at Havard's questions. "When he has polluted the water with alcohol in one glass and nicotine in another one, he takes a little box which contains some kind of insects out of his briefcase. Then he picks up one of them and drops it in the glass of water mixed with alcohol. And what do you think happens?"

"The bug gets drunk," Havard says cheerfully. It is obvious that Armann has managed to get him in a better mood.

"Yes, it possibly feels the effects for a little while, but not for long because it dies."

Havard laughs.

"So when the teacher has explained to the boys just how alcohol affects . . . well, I don't know what he said precisely . . . that this is what happens to insects who drink . . . then . . ."

Havard bursts out laughing and I hear him pour something over the ice in his glass.

"Then he picks up another insect, the same kind as before, and . . ."

"Here's to the bug!" Havard interrupts him.

"Alright, cheers," Armann agrees. While he goes to fetch his glass in the living room he carries on: "So he puts the poor insect into the glass with the nicotine and the same thing happens as when he . . ."

"Drowned the other bug!" Havard adds and laughs.

"Well, at least this creature ends up the same way; it dies of nicotine poisoning. And then there is only the last experiment and, of course, it consists in putting the third insect into the glass with the pure water."

"Armann, I think this friend of yours was having you on," Havard butts in.

"No, no, this last insect just swims around in the water, full of life, and that's the end of the demonstration. Those which landed in the alcohol and nicotine had no chance of survival but the one which landed in the water was still alive when the teacher fished it out, no doubt just to be killed too afterwards."

"So that was the prize for being sensible?" Havard says disgustedly. "Death."

"It at least resulted in my friend Nicholas starting to smoke and drink in his teens; he couldn't bear the thought of having some creepy crawlies swimming around in his intestines."

"Evil shall be swept out with evil, as the saying goes," Havard crows. I can just imagine how this fellow Nicholas appeals to Havard.

"Yes, that's the point," Armann agrees. "Force against force!"

"Steel against steel," Havard adds.

"An eye for an eye," Armann says and giggles like a little boy.

He sounds very relieved now that he has finally told his story, which has taken him half a day to tell me, although he naturally has no idea that he has just done so.

12

I never really liked the lizard—the ancient green lizard or iguana which Orn kept in his study upstairs. He had asked us not to let it out of the room—it often nibbled things that lay on the floor—and he told us especially not to let it into the kitchen; there was always a danger that it could have salmonella. Because of that risk, he added, we should always wash our hands after petting or holding it. I'm quite positive that Havard made a point of taking it into the kitchen, just because Orn had emphatically so asked us not to.

That day—by which I mean the second to last day Havard spent in the house—we took the bus down to Tottenham Court Road at lunchtime. Havard, who was more or less broke after betting heavily the previous weekend, brought the ukulele with him, which he intended to sell back to the shop he had bought it from or perhaps take to another shop on Denmark Street. I had suggested as a joke that he take it down to some underground station and try to strum it there to collect a few coins, and had to literally hold him back when he took the suggestion seriously. However, Havard didn't get as far as trying to do either—selling the instrument or playing it to make money—because he left it on the bus when we got out just next to the Odeon theatre on Tottenham Court Road.

Anyone other than Havard would no doubt have seen the incident as suggesting something like a bad start is a good omen, but, since it was Havard who was involved, the loss of the instrument was rather a taste of what awaited us that day.

While I went into a Virgin Megastore to pick up two CDs I had ordered the week before, Havard waited in a bar on the corner of Oxford Street; he said he needed to cheer himself up after leaving the poor instrument on the bus. Besides, he had already had two beers before lunch and the effect must have started to wear off after the forty minute bus ride.

I spent more time in the record shop than I had intended to. When I entered the bar where Havard was waiting, he was sitting beside an old man in a scruffy raincoat. They were at a narrow table by the wall opposite the bar. There were four empty glasses in front of them, which had clearly contained Guinness, and two smaller ones which had also been emptied. Havard introduced me to the man, who was an old, well-known chess master, and asked me to buy the next round—he had run out of money. He had had to pay for his friend, whom I thought looked like he didn't need any more to drink. I wasn't keen to join them, so I told Havard—in the language that no one understands, least of all he who was not meant to understand it—that I had not come into town just to drink, and told him that I was going to visit more shops. I left him with a ten pound note and some change for the bus fare home. Then I walked down Shaftesbury Avenue and had a beer on my own before going into Ray's Jazz Shop.

While I sat with my cold beer, I began to think that it was incredibly sad that I had left Havard with a penniless drunkard who, at a glance, didn't seem to have anything to offer except that which was enough for Havard: he was a foreigner. Havard always got a kick out of talking to strangers, not least if they originated from a country other than England. No doubt he and this silent chess master were gulping down one more beer or—which I thought was more probable (considering they only had ten pounds to spend)—they had bought some cans of stronger beer and were sitting somewhere in the sun, smoking and drinking, no doubt quite content, at least Havard, to be free from that boring fellow who didn't seem able to relax over a glass of beer.

I had always known that Havard and I would never become very good friends but during the days we spent in London an unbridgeable rift had developed between us. I was the healthy one, the one who had interests and wanted to be constructive, even if just in terms of building a collection of CDs or books; Havard, on the other hand, didn't seem to be interested in anything, unless it was forbidden or contained the highest percentage of alcohol.

I bought him a pack of beer before I set off home later in the afternoon, probably in the hope—at least subconsciously—that he would fall asleep early in the evening. And that's exactly what happened. But I have to admit that the main reason I stopped at the liquor store on the way home was because I had found two CDs in the shop on Shaftesbury Avenue—CDs that I had been looking for for a long time—and I was so childishly happy that I felt I had to celebrate when I got home. Besides the beer for Havard, I bought a flask of whisky and several bottles of beer. However, it was a different sort of happiness that I found when I walked into the house on Brooke Road; Havard had invited his drinking pal home. The curtains were drawn, there was no music on the hi-fi, and the television was off. A thick cloud of tobacco smoke and silent misfortune hung over them.

It only took me five minutes to get rid of Havard's guest; after all the hospitality Havard had shown him, the pitiful man was too weak to show any resistance. Havard protested at first but then realized that it was best to let him go. I had to lead him out of the living room and into the front hall, and I gave him two pounds to help him on his way. I think I also gave him a bottle of beer.

Even though I found out that they had finished a whole bottle of port that I kept in the kitchen, I couldn't be bothered to make a fuss. I expect that I had already decided that I would ask Havard to leave.

After I had hidden the whisky flask and most of the beer, I sat down with Havard and gave him two cans of Special Brew, warning him that he would get no more as he had drunk enough already. Besides, I thought I had made it clear to him that I wouldn't tolerate his behavior any longer; we were really meant to be working here in London—we were getting pocket money that we, of course, had to work for—and already half of the animals who had been entrusted to us were no longer alive. While I shut myself in the living room to listen to my new CDs, I imagined that Havard had finished the beer and gone to bed upstairs. But suddenly, in the middle of Peter Kowald's bass solo, a scream came from the kitchen, and I jumped off the sofa and rushed into the kitchen like a streak of lightning.

If I was beginning to feel the effect of the whisky (which I had smuggled into the living room with me), I think it vanished as soon as I entered the kitchen and saw what had happened. Havard was frozen in the middle of the room and holding a bloody meat knife; on the counter beside the sink lay the lifeless body of the iguana. Although I noticed straightaway that it was considerably shorter than before, I didn't fully understand what had happened until I got nearer and saw its head in the sink. I'm sure that I'll never forget the expression in Havard's eyes when he put down the chopping knife and looked up from the blood-bath: it was like he needed me to protect him from all the evil powers that were threatening him.

I hadn't intended to give him any of my whisky, but when I saw the state that he was in, I told him straightaway to take a swig. After this latest incident in our peculiar household in Stoke Newington, I even had to have a good few mouthfuls and a cigarette to calm down.

I was actually too numb to be angry. Before we cleaned up the mess in the kitchen we sat down in the living room and I tried my best to stay calm, in the hope that Havard would explain why this had happened; really there was no point in getting excited.

He had gone upstairs to bed—I was right there—but he said he couldn't fall asleep because I was playing music so loudly in the living room. He had become restless and thought he would take a look at Ahab in Orn's study. Then he had begun to feel bad in the dark and because—as I knew—he always felt better on the ground floor after dark, he took the lizard down into the kitchen. He needed company (strange though it may sounds in this context), and as the cat only made him feel worse in the dark and I was listening to this weird music of mine, Ahab was the only one he could talk to.

There was nothing to drink in the fridge, so he had had to make do with water. He had put Ahab down on the counter to the right of the sink and while he was waiting for the water to run cold he petted the lizard as he usually did. But on this occasion Ahab didn't like being petted and suddenly—"it was just as if I had been struck by lightning"—bit him. His reaction (that is his neurosis which, of course, had not been improved at all by the amount of alcohol flowing in his blood) was to grab hold of the big chopping knife that hung over the sink. Before he realized what he was doing, he had delivered the fatal blow.

When I recall the incident now, I don't think I realized the gravity of the matter until the following day. Before Havard fell asleep that evening, I tried to make him understand that he could no longer stay in the house; the magnitude of his blunders far outweighed our small responsibilities and so on. I remember that while I tried to get him to understand our situation—or more precisely *my* situation—I felt it was utterly unrealistic. It was almost as if we were on a ship without a captain. Ahab, the captain, was dead, and since the crew could not agree which direction it should take, then half of it—that is the half that had killed off the captain—would have to disembark at the first opportunity. Although Havard was upset, I am not sure he realized the full implications of his deeds. I suspect that he fell asleep without worrying too much, not to mention the fact that the alcohol which he had consumed over the course of the day would have been sufficient to knock out a much bigger creature than him. But when I finally fell asleep in the early hours of the morning, I had made up my mind to kick him out of the house the following day.

He had been up for two or three hours when I awoke at around lunchtime. And it was obvious that he had searched the house high and low for alcohol. He had found the cans of beer, which I had hidden in a bucket in the vacuum cupboard and covered with a smelly floor cloth, and was finishing the third one when I came across him in the kitchen. The cat was there too, hunched over its dish and tearing at the tinned food as earnestly as Havard gulped down the beer. I thought I had prepared him the night before for what I was about to tell him, but he reacted badly, said he was offended, it had been a pitiful accident and the other accident with the rabbit and the guinea pig had come about because he was trying to help them. I said I couldn't be bothered arguing with him, and when I gave him four hundred pounds and told him to leave, his behavior changed instantly. And yet he tried to see how far he could push me. He was obviously already enjoying the money in his imagination when he asked for twice the sum and promised not to show his face again; he smiled as if he had the upperhand in some very important business transaction.

I hadn't looked at the matter from this perspective before, but of course he had taken the model of the whaler *Essex* and the original edition of *Moby-Dick* as some kind of compensation when I refused to accept his offer. Exactly how he had managed to preserve these valuable objects for five years I couldn't possibly understand. Perhaps his loss of the ukulele had taught him to take better care of things; he may have learned something since then, although the conversation that is currently going on in the living room doesn't really give that impression.

13

"But, tell me, Armann, you have a degree in Icelandic, don't you? What does the phrase 'to hold a function *in the house*' mean?" Havard farts and apologizes with a laugh.

"'A function *in the house*,' you say?" Armann sounds as though he has to give this some thought.

"Take this for example: a person has a party in his house, say I have a party here at Emil's place and invite some people, then one doesn't talk about 'having a function *in the house*,' am I right? That is something different, isn't it?"

"Yes . . ." I hear Armann drink, perhaps to jog his memory. Then he clears his throat and tries to explain:

"'To have a function *in the house*' means to have a party, just a normal party, but I suspect that the phrase 'function *in the house*' is more often used in connection with public functions or gatherings that are held by politicians for example, or . . ."

"Oh, I was beginning to think that we were taking part in some gathering *in the house*," Havard interrupts. "That a party *in the house* was perhaps a party that a host held—in this case Emil—without being present; in other words whilst *out of the house*."

"You are such a comedian," Armann says, laughing. At this point the phone rings and Havard answers.

"Hello, who's that?" He is silent for a little while. "My name is Havard. Your name is Vigdis? Emil is unfortunately not at home. No, he hasn't come back. Yes, he came home, but he just hasn't . . . come back again."

Armann giggles.

"Well, it's difficult to say. Perhaps he had to rush out and . . . yes, it looks as though he will be late getting back, at least it seems that way."

Armann giggles again at Havard's comments.

"No, I am just an acquaintance of his," Havard carries on and tells Vigdis his name. "No, I was just coming back from abroad, like Emil, and happened to be passing by. You are in Akureyri, aren't you? No, I . . . yes, Emil told me. He said you were in Akureyri. Yes. Really? What, shall I . . . yes, I'll tell him to phone you. As soon as he comes. OK? Yes, I'll let him know. Auf wiedersehen."

"That was Vigdis," he informs Armann. "The other woman," he adds in a rather insinuating manner.

Havard has just finished talking when the phone rings again. He is probably still holding the receiver, but he seems to wait a little before answering. He clears his throat and says in a husky, masculine voice:

"Guten Tag."

Then he keeps quiet, much longer than he usually does on the telephone, and I imagine that the person on the other end of the line is explaining something to Havard, or takes all that time to introduce himself.

"In a little while?" Havard asks when he finally gets the chance to talk. "She is asleep then? Oh, really? And you are close by here? Yes, he must be coming home any minute now. Yes, yes, at least . . . we'll be here. I just say *willkommen*, madame."

In other words it's Greta. She's tucked her daughter into bed, has probably had a shower, and is on her way over long before I myself am expected. I am rather surprised that Armann doesn't ask who was on the phone and that Havard doesn't mention it to him. No doubt he thinks of Greta as some surprise guest; he is about to treat Armann to an unexpected female visitor.

It is obvious that Armann has been thinking about something else while Havard was talking to Greta. As soon as the phone call ends, Armann points to something he wants him to look at and says:

"That's a rather impressive mustache."

I try to guess which mustache he is referring to. I imagine that he is pointing at the cover of a CD, book, or video, and when Havard says that no decent music can come from such a man, I feel reasonably sure that the man in question is Joe Zawinul.

"Why don't we just carry on with Elvis?" Havard suggests.

"That's up to you," Armann says. "I wasn't thinking of playing this, it was just the face that I thought was rather striking." But he still seems to be thinking of the photo when he suddenly blurts out:

"There is nothing quite so ugly as a handsome man."

"What?" I hear Havard say. "Nothing as ugly as a handsome man? Is *he* a handsome man?"

"I didn't mean that man in particular," Armann answers, and I suddenly see the Austrian pianist from a new, unexpected perspective; he has become a example of masculine good looks.

"But tell me, how can a good looking man be ugly?" I hear Havard fiddling with the CD player. "Am *I* ugly? Would you say I was ugly, for instance?

"I'm not deciding who is ugly and who is handsome. What I am trying to say is that . . ."

"But I am asking you, Armann," Havard interrupts. "Do you think I'm ugly?"

Armann hesitates for a few seconds and then says: "I think you harmonize quite well."

"Harmonize!" Havard doesn't think much of this remark; I have to ask myself what his comment means exactly. "What kind of answer is that, Armann! Does it maybe harmonize? Is it some new grammatical term?"

I have to admit that sometimes I am surprised at Havard's expressions. Perhaps my low opinion of him has blinded me to his ability to express himself, an ability which is of course not confined to the "righteous." If anything, it has more often been used, or abused, to obstruct the progress of righteousness; I consider myself to be a true spokesman for these virtues, at least compared to the misogynist, alcoholic, compulsive gambler, and, most recently, burglar Havard Knutsson (although he hasn't stolen anything since he broke into my flat yet).

"What I was trying to tell you," Armann begins to explain "is that the good looks of the handsome, that is of the most handsome men, very often work against them."

"You're talking about me, then!" Havard bursts out laughing.

"They are isolated by their own beauty, is perhaps a better way to put it," Armann corrects himself. "Not only are their good looks worshipped by others, but they themselves become absorbed in their own admiration. They imagine that their beauty will transport them into some little paradise, but one day, when they are serving a teenager in a fashion shop, they suddenly realize in a flash that they won't get any further; they have reached their peak, serving penniless teenagers in some fashion store."

"No, Armann, now I think you're treading on thin ice. Is there something wrong with working in a fashion shop? For instance, I bought these clothes today and the fellow who sold them to me was nothing spectacular; he wasn't exactly what you would call Mr. Universe."

"It's a fine suit, I must admit, but I don't think you understand me properly," Armann replies. "Tell me something, my good . . . ? Havard, isn't it? Sorry, I'm not very good at remembering names," he says. "It is Havard, isn't it?"

I don't hear any answer and can't quite make out what Havard is doing at the moment.

"But in every other respect I think I can state that I have the memory of an elephant," Armann carries on. "I can remember the birthdays of all the important presidents and kings and, of course, when they died. I even think I remember when your friend Elvis Presley died."

"Talking about elephants," Havard interrupts, "Have you heard the joke about the elephant who stepped on an ant hill? Once upon a time there was this gigantic elephant who came tramping along the river bank."

"Where was that?" Armann enquires, as if the place was of some importance.

"It doesn't matter," Havard says. "Let's just say in India. Then, suddenly, as the elephant is about to have a drink from the stream, he steps on a little ant hill and naturally causes a great commotion for the inhabitants; half of them are killed and those who survive run off to save their lives."

"Which they certainly do," Armann adds.

"Then, while the elephant is drinking from the stream one ant climbs up his leg . . ."

"Crawls up," Armann corrects him.

". . . and a group of his friends . . . that is friends of the ant who was courageous enough to crawl up the elephant until he got as far as the neck. Just imagine: an ant is only so big."

I can just imagine Havard measuring out the size of the ant with his thumb and forefinger.

"And then, when the ant reaches the elephant's neck," he continued, "one of his friends down on the ground, who is crazy with excitement and thirsty for revenge, shouts: 'Strangle him, Emil! Strangle him!'"

"What?" I hear Armann say.

"Strangle him, Emil! Strangle him!" Havard repeats.

I don't know why the name Emil is included in the story, but it is probably because the ant had the same name when I heard the joke some time ago, in primary school. I suspect that the drink is to blame for how long it takes Armann to imagine the tragicomic ant on the broad neck of the elephant (if one can talk about the neck of an elephant). And then—rather quietly to begin with—Armann begins to laugh; he shrieks, like an old, worn out laughter box, it sounds like oil is thrown on a fire or new batteries put in the laughter box. He explodes and between fits of laughter repeats the final sentences of the joke over and over again. I begin to think that he is literally losing his mind, that his mental balance has been endangered by this joke, so that Havard—for the first time in his life—will have to face the consequences of his deeds. But Havard doesn't seem capable of shouldering much responsibility at this point; instead of joining Armann's laughter, he starts imitating the voice of the father in the TV series about Emil at Kattholt. He shouts "Emil!" just like the father shouted when his son had gotten into mischief and was running to lock himself in the woodshed. Havard doesn't just shout once, he carries on almost as if his life depends on it.

I don't quite know if I should laugh or worry; if someone came across the pair of them in the living room right now, they would be sure that both of them were absolutely mad.

"Here, do you think I may help myself to one of those?" Armann asks when he has almost recovered from his fit of laughter. Havard stops shouting abruptly and says yes, he should help himself if he wants one.

"Emil the ant," Armann giggles; the Indian elephant was still on his mind.

"Here's to Emil," Havard says.

"Here's to Emil," Armann says.

They clink their glasses. There is a sound of cellophane, which gets drowned out in the first tones of "Flaming Star" from Elvis Presley. Through the music and the partition I hear Armann groan with pleasure as he has exhales his first puff of cigar smoke.

Part
Three

Heaven's Reward

1

When someone knocks on the front door either Armann or Havard stands up and turns down the music.

"Well, well, do you think it's the master of the house?" Armann says enthusiastically.

"No, Armann, it's the *other* woman," I hear Havard correct him.

"The other woman?" Armann asks, but he gets no answer. Havard has already opened the door.

"Come in," he says, and I can just imagine Greta, tall and dressed in black, perhaps wearing a hat to protect her freshly washed hair from the frost. Her daughter is asleep now in her grandmother's soft bed. Her mother is back and she can't wait to wake up tomorrow morning to play with her new toys from London.

Greta has clearly felt cold on the way; she shudders and says something about the frost on this iceberg, something I have heard myself say under similar circumstances. However, I feel warm inside when I hear her ask if I have come back, and I imagine I detect a hint of concern in her voice. She must have sensed on the bus that I really wanted to see her again, and though Havard has told her that I came home and went straight out again, she is understandably surprised that I'm not here waiting for her. Instead she is invited in by the last man I would want my girlfriend to be introduced to. I am quite shocked when she asks Havard if she has perhaps seen him somewhere before.

"I don't think so," he answers.

"I'm sure I have seen you somewhere before," she repeats, and I say to myself: "Dear God, don't let them know each other." Remember Armann instead, I mumble into the carpet. You must remember him from the plane. One doesn't miss a man like Armann. Just don't recognize Havard, I think to myself.

But it seems certain that she has met Havard at some stage; she repeats that she must have seen him somewhere before, and Havard simply answers that it's possible but he can't remember when that might have been.

"May I take your coat?" he asks. I imagine he puts it on one of the kitchen chairs, as he doesn't bring it into the bedroom.

Greta has obviously come into the living room, as Armann now greets her. He says: "Pleased to meet you," then asks if she is a friend of mine. Before she gets a chance to reply, he says his name is Armann Valur, they met today; I had accidentally taken his glasses with me from the plane we were on together and he had just come a short while ago to fetch them.

"Then we were on the same plane," Greta says cheerfully and sniffs. "Oh, by the way, my name is Greta."

"Pleased to meet you, Greta, My name is Armann Valur," Armann repeats and then asks: "But tell me, were you and Emil on the same plane?"

"You and I must have been on the same plane. If you were on the same plane as Emil, then we were traveling together," Greta answers, and I say to myself that she has a pretty voice. It's warm and provocative at the same time—not at all thin and self-conscious, like Vigdis's voice, for instance.

"Then you weren't *with* Emil, were you?" Armann carries on in disbelief.

"Not like that, no," Greta answers. She obviously seems to find this misunderstanding amusing. "Or I mean, yes of course I was *with* him on the plane today. And with you too."

"Are we perhaps expecting more passengers from this flight?" Havard interrupts ironically and asks Greta if she would like something to drink, if he can bring her anything. She says that she brought a bottle of red wine, but maybe he could offer her a strong drink first, something to put a bit of warmth into her body, perhaps cognac if there is any.

"No problemo," Havard answers, and I'm quite certain that the phrase "to put a bit of warmth into her body" awakens some unseemly thoughts in his mind as he fetches the cognac.

"But tell me, Greta," Armann continues, suddenly becoming very formal, "Did you come back from London today?"

Greta laughs amiably; I would laugh with her if I could.

"Clever boy, Armann!" Havard calls from the kitchen, and I gather from Greta's next comment that she doesn't think it is right to tease Armann—an older man whom she has never met before—any more.

"Yes, I was just returning from London," she says seriously; she is letting Armann know that he was right.

"So we were all returning from London," Armann says. He seems to have understood the situation at last.

"Emil and I were once together in London," Havard informs them, and I beg him not to say any more. But of course Havard can't hear a man who doesn't speak out loud and is, on top of everything else, under the bed in the next room. I, on the other hand, can hear him quite well when he goes into the living room (probably with a glass of cognac for Greta) and mentions the very subject which I was just—in my silent way—begging him not to discuss.

"We were looking after a whole house in London," he says, as if he expects to be rewarded with the undivided attention of the listeners. "And not just a whole house, four little animals too."

Why on earth don't I do something? What is wrong with me? What reason do I have for lying here under my own bed while these two men (one of them just released, or escaped, from some kind of institution in Sweden, the other, who should have been long gone, having come to collect his glasses) behave as if they are at home here; it seems as though they *are* at home, in my very own flat. The only reason I don't do anything is because it is too late. Now that Greta has arrived—this woman whom I have adored from a distance for nearly fifteen years and got to know by some amazing coincidence—I am not going to crawl out from under the bed and show myself—on the very day that promised to be one of the better days of my life—as the wretched coward that the day's events have turned me into.

"Then you weren't on the plane today?" Greta asks with a laugh.

"I was just having a look around Reykjavik," Havard answers. "I have just come home from Sweden myself."

"From Lund, by any chance?" Armann asks.

"Lund!" Havard almost spits the word out. "What the hell would I want to do in Lund!"

"Lund is in Sweden. You said you were in Sweden."

I can't decide whether Armann is teasing Havard, and maybe trying to get a little revenge after being called a *clever boy*, but as a result Havard's stay in Sweden and London is not discussed any further. Greta begins to talk about the strange names of towns in Sweden; she mentions some name that I don't catch, and when Armann adds a few more and tells them that he has been to a language conference in Uppsala, Greta shows interest and the conversation veers too far from Havard for him to bring it back down to his level. He keeps quiet for a little while and though I'm fully aware of how much alcohol he can consume, I start hoping that he is getting tired.

"But what about you, my comrade Havard, were you studying there in Sverige?" Armann asks after Greta mentions that she attended an arts course on some island in Sweden.

"I'm *comrade* Havard, now am I?" Havard is offended and sounds as if he is feeling rather isolated. "No, comrade Armann, men like me don't have any need for education."

Without having formed an exact plan, I begin to imagine that Greta could help me, that I could possibly let her know that I'm here without giving her too much of a fright, and she could find a feasible way to get rid of Havard and Armann. If she went to the toilet, I could perhaps get her attention by whistling quietly. I know it is risky—she might get frightened and scream—but if it worked I could ask her to find me a piece of paper and a pen, and then I would pass her a message when she re-emerged from the toilet. It's also possible that I could slide out from under the bed for a second and fetch pen and paper, somehow catch Greta's attention when, sooner or later, she goes to the toilet, and give her instructions on how best to get rid of our inopportune guests.

2

Now, when I think back to the party in Hjalmholt fifteen years ago, where Greta disappeared into the children's bedroom, I put myself in the shoes of that boy my age whom I have always envied for his experience that evening, even though I suspect that he was too drunk to remember it properly. But there is always the possibility that nothing happened; that the boy was too drunk to rise up to the expectations of the blonde super girl (as I imagined her) and that she had mussed up her hair and reddened her cheeks herself, to give the impression that something remarkable had taken place under, or on top of, the child's soft duvet. I have sometimes asked myself why I wasn't the one to spend that half hour with her in the children's bedroom, but today, as I finally get to know Greta, I am really glad that we haven't met before. If that had happened, she wouldn't be standing in my flat now; we would probably have said hello on the plane, maybe chatted a little (not mentioning the previous meeting), and then said goodbye without arranging to meet again in the evening. That's how I imagine it anyway.

But then it's a question of whether it would have been more fun to have the memory of a wonderful half hour in bed with this girl, or to have her come to meet me at my flat, while I'm hiding under a bed in a room that a child uses several weeks a year.

"Didn't Emil say when he was going to come back?" Greta asks when Armann mentions that he is hungry and that they should find something to eat.

"I haven't heard from him at all," Havard answers and adds that something must have happened, it looks as if I had rushed out in a hurry.

"But you said you were expecting him any minute, didn't you?"

"I thought so, yes."

"But it must be quite a while since he came home. He did mention that he had to stop somewhere in the taxi on the way home, but he said he was just going to relax at home after the flight."

"Well, he called me at least," Armann comments, and I seem to hear him stand up; he groans with the exertion. "He left a message on my answering machine and told me about my glasses."

I am in the process of turning over on my side—I am extremely tired of lying on my stomach—when Armann comes into the hall, puffing and panting like he has just come in from a long walk. I roll back on to my stomach, lift the sheet slightly up from the floor, and see him go into the bathroom. He has taken his cigar with him (which is no doubt the reason for his heavy breathing) and puts it down, still smoking, on the edge of the sink while he gets ready to urinate. I can hear that Greta and Havard are still wondering where I have gone. She suggests that I have gone to visit my parents, but Havard rules that out because of the telephone call from my mother.

"Something must have happened," Greta says. "I think it's rather strange that he hasn't let me know, we had agreed that I should come here to meet him."

"Yes, I think so too," Havard says. "I expected him to be at home, it's not every day that *I* am in Iceland."

"He must turn up," Greta says, trying to make it sound as though there is no reason to despair. "He can't have gone far, at least."

I am here, Greta, I whisper under my breath, though there is no reason to whisper as Armann is making so much noise as he urinates that it probably drowns out all talking. I resist the temptation to watch him, let the sheet fall carefully to the floor, and decide to change my position until Armann comes out. But he suddenly shouts "Damn it!" and I lift the sheet a little to see what is going on. The first thought that comes to mind is that he has bumped into the burning cigar, but when I look at him there is no mistaking the fact that he has pissed over the edge of the toilet; he is holding his penis with one hand and looking down at his pants and wiping them with his other hand. I lift the sheet up slightly higher and can see his face; he is frowning and muttering something in a huff.

"What's going on?" Havard calls from the living room.

"There is some damn puddle here on the floor," Armann answers, as if the bathroom doesn't quite meet his hygiene requirements.

"You should take more care not to pee on the floor," Havard shouts, and I'm glad that Greta doesn't laugh at his pathetic joke. "You will flush the toilet, won't you?" he carries on, as if he is doing his best to make Greta laugh, but she isn't amused, or—as is likely—she doesn't think Havard's comments are funny in the least.

Either Armann shuts out Havard's comments or he is too busy wiping his pants and shoes with my towel. In any case, he doesn't reply. When he has flushed the toilet and put down the towel beside the sink, he calls out to the others in the living room that it might be time for them to eat something. I get the feeling that they—Armann, Havard and Greta—are the ones who live here and that I am at the most some sort of insect, some dust mite that has fallen onto the floor from the sheet and will be sucked up in a few days when Greta orders Havard to get out the hoover. I really want to slide out from under the bed and grab hold of Armann's leg when he comes out of the bathroom— this impossible situation is getting on my nerves again—but he still has something left to do. Instead of washing his hands, he begins to examine his face in the mirror, and I can see him begin to squeeze a spot or a wart on one of his nostrils.

Armann's suggestion seems to go unnoticed. I hear Havard say something about music. Since Armann is in the bathroom, I imagine that he will play something that he has chosen himself, no doubt to please the lady.

"I don't mind," Greta says, and it becomes obvious—contrary to what I expected—that Havard suggested they play some Viennese waltzes, probably my Janos Ferencsik edition. I imagined that he would carry on with Elvis Presley, but I wouldn't be surprised if Greta's presence had influenced his choice.

"Maybe it's too loud," he says, and though I don't hear Greta agree, the volume is lowered, almost down to nothing.

I don't see if Armann succeeds in squeezing the spot on his face, but suddenly, as he starts whistling along to "The Blue Danube," he has a comb in his hand—which probably came out of his pocket; I don't own a comb myself—and he runs it through his tobacco-colored hair, from his forehead down to the nape of his neck. He seems to be having trouble getting his hair to stay in place, so he wets it with water from the tap, tries again, and seems to have more success this time. Then he puts the comb in the side pocket of his jacket, bares his teeth at the mirror, and walks out of the bathroom.

"Now I wouldn't mind getting one of those food trays that we had on the plane," he says on the way into the living room. "Wouldn't that be good, Greta dear?" he adds, like he's addressing his wife.

Greta says that she isn't hungry enough to want airplane food and she thinks that they should wait for me, if they are thinking of eating at all. She then gets the idea that I probably have a cell phone and suggests that we try to find out, I must have one on me. While she phones information and asks for the cell phone number of Emil S. Halldorsson, I try to remember where I left my phone. I took it out of my jacket pocket when I came in, but I can't for the life of me remember where I put it. I expect it is in the kitchen or the living room, but then it starts ringing here in the bedroom. I remember now: I put it down beside the computer when I was looking at my email.

"Where is the ringing coming from?" Greta asks excitedly, as if she expects the telephone to tell them where I am.

Which it actually does.

Havard doesn't take long to track down the sound; he rushes into the bedroom and grabs the phone.

"Emil here," he says in a gruff voice.

Greta doesn't answer him. Instead she comes into the bedroom and switches the cordless phone off. I'm relieved that I didn't have my cell phone on me.

"I don't find this at all amusing, to tell you the truth," Greta complains. "I'm beginning to fear that something has happened to him."

"It's not a bad phone," Havard answers. I'd give it to him if he would just get out of my home.

"What about his father?" Greta asks. "Do his parents live together?"

"That I can't tell you," Havard says. "But, I found the number of his father Halldor today and his mother answered the phone."

As soon as Greta sits down at the foot of the bed, right above my head, she asks Havard to call my mother to find out if I have gone there. The mattress sinks down uncomfortably close to my head and just misses touching me. Havard tells her that my mother has already called, and then Greta asks whether he knows of some friend I could have gone to visit. "We can't stay in his flat all evening, you can't finish all his wine, I mean, he has only just gotten home from abroad."

"*We?*" Havard seems to be rather offended. "Who are *we?*"

"I mean all of us," Greta says apologetically.

"I don't know any of Emil's friends," Havard says. "I haven't seen him for a long time, we never really knew each other very well."

"You do *know* him, don't you?" Greta seems to grow suspicious.

"Of course I know him. We were in London together. We also worked in the same place."

"And was he expecting you here today? Did you speak to him first?"

Armann's whistling drowns out the quiet waltz in the living room; "Künstlerleben" is just about to begin.

"Well, he didn't really know that I was coming, I just came home from Sweden unexpectedly. It wasn't really planned at all." I hear him press on the keyboard.

"What were you doing in Sweden?" Greta asks. "Hey, you shouldn't read his email," she adds accusingly.

"I'm not doing much at the moment. You mean am I working or something like that?"

"Stop reading his email," Greta repeats angrily.

"I'm not reading it, I'm just . . ." He is interrupted by my cell phone, which starts ringing. The first person I think of is Saebjorn; he's the only person I know who prefers to call a cell phone number before a home number, even though he knows that I am at home. "Hey, now he's calling!" Havard shouts. "He's seen that someone has called him from here."

Oh yes? I say to myself, and Greta makes a similar comment; she asks if he really thinks so.

"Emil?" Havard seems convinced that it's me. "Hello? Who is that? Saebjorn? Yes, this is Emil's place. It is Emil's. Who am I? I am Havard."

I can feel Greta move her behind around on the bed, and then I hear her pick up something from my son Halldor's toy box. It sounds like she is looking at a fire engine I gave him last summer.

"Yes, Saebjorn, I think so. I think he just nipped out. Yes, yes, do that . . ."

Greta lets out a sound, as if she has pricked herself on something, and for a moment I feel as if it is I who has hurt myself, that she has sat further in on the bed and made the springs poke into the back of my neck. She probably pinched her finger in the ladder on the fire engine; I have done it myself.

"Vigdis?" Havard asks in surprise. "No, it isn't Vigdis. It's Greta, Emil's friend. What? Do you want to talk to her? No, alright. Yes, I think he'll be back soon. Shall I tell him you called? No, probably just out to the shop, but he has been rather long. Yes, just knock, we are here looking after his house. OK? Alright, Saebjorn. Goodbye, Saebjorn."

"Who is Vigdis?" Greta asks.

"Emil seems to know some girl called Vigdis," Havard answers, and I beg him, for God's sake, not to say any more about it. "How did you manage to hurt yourself on that?" he asks, and I'm really thankful that he steers the subject away from Vigdis.

"I pinched myself," Greta answers.

"Hey, I want to show you something in the other room," Havard says. I imagine he is going to show her the ship and the book.

He stands up from the computer table, and, as he goes towards the door, I get ready to make the most of the opportunity and tap Greta on her foot while she's still sitting on the bed. But just when Havard goes out of the room, Greta stands up, and before I can do anything it is too late to touch her. I curse myself for being so slow, but I am convinced that it would be less risky to try to get her attention when she goes to the toilet by herself, which she must do soon.

I think back to our first conversation in front of the toilet on the plane. If we get to know each other better (that is when this nightmare is over) that trip to the toilet will be a shared memory of our first conversation.

"I was beginning to think that you had both gone," Armann says when they come into the living room. I haven't heard much from him, apart from the occasional whistle to the Viennese waltzes. He seems to have forgotten that he was hungry.

"Here's what I want to show you," Havard says eagerly. "See here, isn't she beautiful?"

"Is she your daughter?" Greta sounds surprised.

"Don't you think she is pretty?"

"Yes, she's a very pretty girl. How old is she?"

"She's . . . what . . . she'll be eight this summer."

I had no idea that Havard was a father. I don't even know if I should be happy for him, I haven't a clue about the circumstances in which the poor child was conceived.

"She is very pretty, Havard," Greta repeats.

For some reason I feel I can believe what Greta is saying, even though she seems to be something of a tease. It's no doubt because I trust her; she is the only sensible person in here—apart from myself, that is. If she says that Havard's daughter is pretty, then I believe that she is pretty. But I still find it difficult to accept the fact that he has a daughter.

"May I see, Havard?" Armann says, though I can't imagine he is very interested in children.

3

"Is she holding a Bible?" Armann asks, and Havard sounds rather annoyed when he answers:

"Yes, is there anything wrong with that?"

"Absolutely not. The Bible is as good as any other book," Armann says and adds that she is a pretty girl.

"Was the photo taken abroad?" Greta asks. "The atmosphere seems to be so foreign somehow, especially those heavy dark curtains in the background. Was it taken in America?"

"In America?" Havard hesitates for a moment and then tells Greta that yes, the photo was taken there; the girl's mother, with whom he no longer lives—understandably, I say to myself—had gone off to America with the girl, but he sees her now and again. She visits him regularly, last time in Sweden.

Sounds likely, I think to myself.

But I think it is very strange that Havard never mentioned his family to me. If his daughter is nearly eight, she must have been two or three when we were in London. Now I recall that he told me once that he didn't have any children; that children were better off without a father like him, as I think he put it.

"Well, my friends," Armann barks after Havard has told them about his daughter and her mother. "One can't just survive on photos. Isn't it time we had something to eat?"

"What's the matter, aren't you happy here, Armann?" Havard asks, as if he is addressing a little child. "Didn't I give you coffee and cognac. You had a cigar too, and can have another if you want. You just came here to fetch your glasses. Don't you think it is a bit much to suddenly expect food?"

Good fellow, I think to myself and mentally thank Havard for putting Armann in his place, even though I suspect it was done to impress Greta.

"Havard, my good fellow," Armann says, "I don't mean to sound ungrateful for what you have offered here . . ."

"What *Emil* has offered," Havard butts in.

"Yes, what our friend Emil has offered here," Armann says and is again interrupted by Havard, who suddenly starts singing:

"*Where the Lord provides / blessings come from above . . .*"

Greta laughs; she seems to recognize the hymn.

"I am not talking about a four-course meal or anything like that," Armann adds. Havard carries on singing:

"*Where holy words are recited / there is heavenly peace and love.*"

These religious words don't seem to make any impression on Armann; he is more interested in finishing what he is trying to say: "I was only wondering if Emil had a little something in the freezer that we could heat up. It is not very sensible to drink on an empty stomach, you know that, Havard."

I'm not so sure that Havard does know it. At Brooke Road his breakfast consisted of two or three large cans of Carlsberg Special Brew, and normally he didn't eat anything solid until later in the day, out of dire necessity. He doesn't seem to bother answering Armann, and leaves it to Greta to find a solution to the problem.

"Why don't you just run out to the sweet shop?" she suggests.

"Sweet shop, you say?" He is upset; he hadn't expected this kind of reaction. "Once it was called a confectioner's, if I remember correctly."

There is a knock on the front door.

"Have a look out the window and see who it is!" Havard calls out in a whisper, no doubt to Greta, and before they find out who it is, there is another knock.

"I don't think it's Emil," I hear Greta say in the same kind of loud whisper.

"Wait a moment then," Havard says in a warning tone. "Don't open straight away."

I hear him go into the living room. Armann asks him what he is doing; Havard signals to him to keep quiet and comes, almost running, into the bedroom, where he puts something down on the floor near the toy box. The knocking continues. Havard rushes out again; it sounds as though he slides on the floor when he goes into the hall. He pauses to catch his breath before he opens the front door.

The person outside—clearly a man, judging from his voice—says something I can't hear and Havard answers:

"Yes, that's me."

I can feel cold, fresh air flow in along the hall and into the room. I recognize Jaime's voice straight away; he asks if I have come home yet, and Havard says no but why doesn't he come in.

Although I had told Jaime and Saebjorn about my stay in London with Havard, I have no idea if they remember his name. I got to know Saebjorn shortly after I came home from that trip and Jaime about two years ago, so we have never really spoken about him.

Jaime says good evening to Greta and Armann and they return his greeting. I'm impatient to find out what it is that Havard ran into the bedroom with before he opened the door, and I wriggle a little in the direction of Halldor's toy box in order to get closer to it. I pull it carefully in my direction with my left foot; the dust gets stirred up with each movement I make and settles on my face like a cement.

"Are you the Spaniard?" Armann asks cheerfully, as if they are waiting to complete a group and only the Spaniard is missing. "We are here, Emil's flight companions, all we need is our pal, Emil."

"Were you on the plane with him?" Jaime asks.

"Yes, we were," Armann answers proudly. "Not *him* though," he adds. No doubt he means Havard, who takes over:

"I was just coming from Sweden. You know: Sverige. Volvo. Abba."

"So everyone has come from abroad, it seems," Jaime says—I can just imagine his boyish smile—and then he corrects Armann: "I'm not really Spanish, I come from Chile."

"That's even better," Armann says. "It's not every day one talks to—how is it again—*un chileno*, isn't it?"

"*Si: un chileno.* You have obviously learned some Spanish."

"No, I haven't," Armann answers, almost as if Jaime's praise was an insult.

Behind the toy box I discover the sailing ship and the book. I don't have to wonder much about Havard's reason for removing the objects from the living room; of course he doesn't want my friends to find out who he is, at least not while he is the host here (if one can speak in those terms). He naturally assumes that I have told them all about him, and he hopes that they won't recognize him. With some difficulty I manage to reach the book with my foot, but I get a terrible pain in my hip; it feels like I've strained something, which wouldn't surprise me after lying here for so long. Normally I would shout out in pain, but with the discipline and concentration I have been forced to master the past few hours, I'm able—admirably I think—to suppress the shout.

It feels rather special to be handling the book again. I think that Orn paid around five thousand pounds for it. And though he didn't let me suffer in any way on account of its disappearance from his collection, just the same I suspected all along that Havard sold it for a song in some second-hand bookshop. I put the book on the carpet in front of me and find the first page of the story:

Call me Ishmael.

By removing the letters *s*, *h*, and *a* from the name Ishmael, one is left with the anagram of my name: *Imel.* And the removed letters form another anagram for the English word *ash.* I smile to myself. Without intending to take these word games too seriously, I think first of the word cremation and then the thing for which I would almost be ready to give this original edition of *Moby-Dick*: a cigarette. White, new, and fresh smelling from the carton on the table in the living room. When I glance quickly over the first chapter, I recall the first time I read the book many years ago. As I approach the end of the chapter, my eye pauses automatically at the word *horror.* I read the whole paragraph and get the feeling that the contents are appropriate at this point in my life:

Not ignoring what is good, I am quick to perceive a horror, and could still be social with it—would they let me—since it is but well to be on friendly terms with all the inmates of the place one lodges in.

All of a sudden there is a sound of breaking glass. I hear Havard swear and then Jaime declines a drink when Havard says that he had intended to give him whisky, but he had just let the glass slip to the floor.

"There are more glasses," Armann says, but Jaime insists that he doesn't want anything to drink, he can't really stop, he has just come to see if I had brought back the CD he had asked me to buy. To tell the truth I am quite surprised; I did buy him a CD—exactly the one he asked for and it took me some time to find it—but I understood that both he and Saebjorn were going to come and have a drink and chat with me this evening. Of course I am aware that I don't seem to be there, but I think Jaime could at least wait for Saebjorn, who is bound to come any minute now.

"Can't I offer you a little red wine?" Greta says. I nod on Jaime's behalf. I can imagine that Greta would like him to stay for a little while; in a way it must give her more hope that I will turn up.

"Thanks, maybe just one glass," Jaime says after a little thought.

"Of course, you prefer wine down there in Chile, don't you?" Armann asks. He seems to be very pleased that Jaime is staying.

"Yes, perhaps," Jaime answers. "Emil was on the plane today wasn't he?" he asks with a laugh. I am rather astonished at this stupid question; the CDs didn't come by themselves.

"Oh yes," Armann answers. "We were all traveling with God today; Emil, Greta here and I . . ."

"Wait a minute," Greta interrupts from the kitchen, where I imagine she is opening the red wine bottle. "Who was traveling with God?"

"Well, weren't we? Weren't we on the un-explorable path high above civilization today? On *God's path* as our friends in the church say."

"Don't count me in, for God's sake," interjects Havard, who sounds rather tired.

"But, on the other hand, I have never understood what is so un-explorable about God's path, as they say," is heard from Armann. "It's not until we come down to earth that we begin to get lost. Take today for example; no sooner had we landed in Keflavik than my glasses were lost. Then I was led all over the airport building until I was completely lost and had no hope of finding my way at all."

"Is it possible that it had something to do with the loss of your glasses?" Havard asks and Greta laughs in the kitchen.

At almost the same moment as she pulls the cork out of the red wine bottle, the phone rings; it seems to be in the kitchen too.

"I'll get it," Greta calls, but she has to ask Jaime to help her to get the connection.

"Good evening," she says. "Yes, this is Emil's place. On Grettisgata, yes. Hello, I'm Greta. No, they are just Emil's friends." It's obvious that the person on the other end of the line—whom I guess is my mother—can hear male voices coming from the living room. "Yes, there is also a man who was on Emil's flight today, I think he came to fetch his glasses. What? Me? No, I'm just Emil's girlfriend. Since *when*? What do you mean? I'm just his girlfriend."

She sounded rather annoyed just then and I begin to suspect who she is talking to.

"No, he has obviously left his cell phone here at home," Greta continues. "No, I have no idea where he has gone. Yes. No. Eh? Yes, I'll tell him to phone as soon as he arrives. At the hotel? He knows where it is? Alright. Goodbye."

"Well!" Greta says to herself when she hangs up.

"Who was that, then?" Armann asks. "It certainly wasn't Emil."

"No, it was some Vigdis," Greta answers.

4

She says she is at the hotel. Vigdis, who is now just *some* Vigdis. Most probably she called from the reception or the pay phone in the foyer, but I imagine her in one of the bedrooms, lying on a double bed, still holding the receiver in her hand; she has made up her mind about what this Greta is doing at my place. Vigdis could be in the same room where we (Halldor, my son, she and I) stayed last summer, in the suite that she booked for us. She is telling herself what a pathetic little shit I am—wondering why I can't call to let her know that I have met someone else, and why she has to go to the trouble of calling herself, just to have this new girlfriend of mine answer.

No doubt she has given up all hope of getting the clothes she asked me to buy. She probably imagines that I bought them for her but have given them to this new girlfriend—this new girlfriend who is so blatantly lying when she says that she doesn't know where I am. Of course she knows nothing about the bottle of cognac and the box of chocolates. But the bottle is no longer presentable as a gift, and I suddenly realize how hopeless it is to give her the box of chocolates; it would be the same as buying her a banana and a bottle of ginger ale. I guess that she is wearing her black hotel skirt at this moment; she lies with her legs sprawled out on the bed and curses the memories that the room holds for us.

The music has been changed. In place of Viennese waltzes, I hear Arthur Blythe blow his horn above a strange combination of tuba and bongo drums; Jaime has chosen this. He turns up the volume a bit, and I hear Havard complain about something. Then Greta says that it sounds just fine.

Vigdis invited Halldor and me north to Akureyri one weekend last summer. She had just started working in the hotel, and Halldor and I were quite surprised when she met us at the airport and told us that she had booked the suite for us; she got it with some staff discount. I had just been telling Halldor that she worked in a very fine hotel in Akureyri, but I had imagined that we would stay in the room she rented in the town center.

Our weekend up north was in many ways quite memorable, especially for little Halldor. Amongst other things, we counted the steps leading up to the church and got a different number than we had been told was right; we visited Nonni's House; and we went to meet some relatives of mine whom I hadn't seen for ten years. On Saturday, Vigdis gave Halldor a game—a beautiful, well-made wooden box with marbles in it—which I suggested he keep at Grettisgata because it was so big. He was allowed to make the final decision though, and he took the game with him when he returned to Denmark three weeks later. The climax of the weekend, at least for Halldor, was when we went out on Eyjafjord in a speedboat with a waiter from the hotel, a man of about forty. I heard just before Christmas that the waiter had hanged himself in the hotel laundry room; he had been betrayed by a woman who happened to work there.

When I called Halldor last New Year to wish him a "Happy New Year," I told him that the man in the boat had hanged himself in the hotel, the same hotel that we had stayed in. I know I wouldn't have mentioned it to him if I hadn't been drinking, and I really regretted doing so when Anna, his mother, called me later on New Year's day to scold me for telling a six-year-old child stories of suicides.

These three days up north left an almost uncomfortably strong family feeling, especially in Vigdis's mind, I think. The whole time we were together I could see in Halldor's eyes that he felt he would never be a real part of it. I remember Vigdis saying "We must meet again more often" to both of us when we said goodbye at the airport. I don't think Halldor would have objected; he seemed to like my girlfriend, although I can never decide if I want our relationship to become more serious. And now that a strange girl answered Vigdis on my phone, I am rather afraid that our relationship is about to end. After the weekend at the hotel in July, we met several times before New Year, mostly in Reykjavik, but this year we have only spoken over the phone. I was beginning to hope that Vigdis's feelings, which she displayed so openly when Halldor and I were visiting, were cooling down.

While I imagine Greta, instead of Vigdis in the hotel room up north, I am quite sure that she knows that the caller was my girlfriend. She has probably decided not to make any excuses and thought that since I wanted to meet her—even though I had a girlfriend and hadn't turned up where we had agreed to meet—she at least has the right to call herself my girlfriend, more of a right than some woman with whom I probably had a relationship earlier, someone from my past. I can't deny that Greta is very much in the present, especially now that I have undressed both of us in my mind and we are in an imaginary hotel room, no longer in Akureyri. I have checked us into a hotel here in Reykjavik, one which has no connection whatsoever with Vigdis. We are going into the bathroom together, the steam from the hot shower has made the mirror as useless as I am here under the bed, and then there is another knock on the front door.

Armann is convinced that it is me. "Better late than never," he says cheerfully but when it becomes apparent that it is not the person he expected, he refers to the proverb that some people never seem to turn up.

Jaime opens the door to Saebjorn, and one of the others stretches over to the stereo and turns down the volume. Saebjorn starts by asking Jaime why he didn't phone him before coming and is very surprised to hear that I haven't come home yet.

"Well, what is all this then?" Saebjorn asks once the door is closed; I can feel the pleasant fresh air that they have allowed to enter. I expect he means all the people he doesn't know and the wine on the table and the cigarette smoke that I imagine is already very thick, since I'm beginning to breathe it in the bedroom. "Is there a party here and Emil isn't even at home?"

"Excuse me, who are you?" Havard asks. He obviously doesn't like my friend's accusing tone.

"Who am I?"

"Yes, who are you?"

"That depends on who is asking."

"Oh, is that so! So who *you* are depends on who *I* am?"

"Come on!" Greta interrupts to prevent unnecessary ill feeling. "Can't you just introduce yourselves?"

"My name is Havard Knutsson," Havard says with cold formality.

"Armann Valur here."

"Havard?" I hear Saebjorn say. It sounds like he recognizes the name.

"I'm Greta."

"I spoke to you earlier," Saebjorn says. He seems to be talking to Havard. "My name is Saebjorn, I called earlier."

"OK, that wasn't so difficult," Havard answers.

"But what is going on here?" Saebjorn carries on asking. "Where is Emil? Why hasn't he come home?"

"If only we knew," Armann answers.

"We are all waiting for him," Greta says, and Havard tries to explain why they are all here.

"I came here this afternoon, it must have been around . . ."

"But how do you know him?" Saebjorn interrupts.

"How do we know each other? We are just old friends. But anyway, I came late this afternoon and knocked and there was nobody home. Then I looked in the window and saw that there was water boiling on the stove so I crawled in through the window and turned off the burner."

"When was that?" Jaime asks.

"Around five or six o'clock."

"And hasn't he been back since?" Saebjorn asks.

It is beginning to sound like a murder interrogation. The difference is that the body is still breathing; it has followed the investigation from the start.

"We are just waiting for him," Havard says. "I saw that he had just come home from abroad, the suitcases have been emptied and of course I thought that he had just nipped out. I mean, he can't have gone far, he has just been delayed. I can't see that it's so unusual."

"But I mean . . ." Saebjorn is clearly not satisfied with the explanation he gets from my unknown friend here, but really he has no cause to disbelieve him. "Haven't you tried to find him? Doesn't he have his cell phone with him?"

"He left it here in the flat," Greta answers. "It has been ringing all the time, hasn't it?" I imagine that the question is addressed to Havard and that it is he who answers.

"I think everyone has been trying to contact him. Both of you, of course, then his mother and some Vigdis. Is she his fiancée?"

"Is she his fiancée!" Saebjorn is clearly still very suspicious of my friendship with Havard. "Wait a moment, aren't you friends? Didn't you say you were old friends?"

"Has that got anything to do with his fiancée?" Havard objects. "I have just come from Sweden where I have been living for several years; how am I to know what Emil's fiancée is called?"

I can't remember if I had told Saebjorn and Jaime that Havard was in Sweden; from what I can hear, they don't seem to have any notion of who he is. On top of everything else it bothers me to hear them talking about Vigdis as my fiancée in front of Greta. From my point of view—however ridiculous it is in these circumstances—Vigdis and I aren't engaged in any way, though she might think of us in those terms.

"Alright, alright," Saebjorn says. "You just have to understand that I find it rather strange coming here and there is no Emil around."

"Of course it is strange," Havard agrees, no doubt glad that his presence in my home has finally been accepted. "Can't you imagine how strange I thought it was to come here and there was no Emil, just boiling water?"

"But, I mean, the man returns from abroad today," Saebjorn continues, "and when one comes to visit him there is nothing here but his luggage! And the wine he bought has been opened . . . it's his wine, isn't it?"

"Actually I brought this bottle," Greta says, but apart from the red wine, Saebjorn is quite right. Alcohol isn't exactly the thing I regret most at this instant, though.

"It's just as if he has misbehaved and run off to the woodshed," Havard says and laughs, as if he is trying to relieve the tension in the room. "Just like his namesake at Kattholt."

I can't imagine that Saebjorn finds this comment very funny.

"Yes, or just like the ants that the elephant trod on," Armann adds with a giggle.

"And how do you know each other?" Saebjorn asks, like he wants to get rid of every trace of doubt from his mind.

"We were with Emil on the way home," Armann answers.

"We were on the same plane today," Greta explains.

"I really just came to fetch my glasses and . . . wait a minute, that's right; he called me after he got here, so it's at least clear that he *came* home."

"Was that ever a question?" Havard asks, obviously annoyed with the linguist.

"So he called you?" Saebjorn asks.

"Most probably as soon as he got in," Armann answers.

Greta offers Saebjorn a glass of red wine, and when he has accepted—rather sulkily it seems—Greta tells Armann to look at the table.

"Look, you have spilled ash over everything on the table," she says.

"I?" Armann sounds surprised, almost as if he has been accused of some terrible crime.

"You miss the ashtray every time, I've noticed."

It is difficult for me to tell whether Greta is joking or is seriously asking the culprit to wipe all the ash off the table. I'm not really worried about the books and the CDs anymore, not now that Jaime and Saebjorn have arrived.

"Armann doesn't smoke," Havard says. "He told me he never smokes."

"You must clean up the table," Greta says to Armann, but I don't hear his reply because Jaime and Saebjorn drown out his voice—they're discussing the rest of the things lying on the table: the books, videos, and music.

Amongst the books which I bought in London is a recent account of the fate of the whaler *Essex*. Though I don't expect that it will be a likely subject of discussion in the living room, it is even more unlikely that Havard will try to show my friends the model ship and the original edition of *Moby-Dick*. Yet I don't think it is wise to keep the book under my bed any longer. I close it, move it as far as I can down past my body, and push it behind the toy box, alongside the carved whaler.

5

"So you are all interested in music?" I hear Havard comment. I can just imagine that Jaime and Saebjorn have separated themselves from the others, though the living room doesn't offer much space for privacy in the crowd that has gathered. They are probably discussing the things that I brought back. Somehow I would have thought that Saebjorn—or both of them, Saebjorn and Jaime—would try to find out more about me, but at the moment they don't seem to be very worried.

"Listen, I'm going to phone Emil's mother," Saebjorn says, almost as if he is answering me.

"So, was Emil buying you some CDs?" Havard asks. "He's a good guy, Emil. Quite solid."

Thanks Havard. It sounds like Saebjorn is standing up; he says he is going to check on her, meaning my mother most probably. He asks where the phone is and Greta finds it for him.

"What did he bring you this time?" Havard continues and interrupts Jaime who is about to answer. "Just now Armann and I were playing . . . what was it again, Armann? What were we playing just now, Armann, that classical CD?"

Saebjorn has come into the bedroom. He sits down in the middle of the bed, which sags under the weight of his long body without making the springs poke down into me, and he begins to turn over the pages of a book, which I immediately recognize as the telephone directory—the pages sound so thin. Then he mutters my father's name as he turns the pages over, one after another, and just as I'm about to tap on his heel, Armann appears in the doorway. He makes a rather strange surprised sound, excuses himself and says he meant to go to the bathroom. He has clearly had too much to drink.

"Armann! What's the name of the music we were playing just now, the classical disc?" Havard shouts from the living room.

"The classical disc?" Armann shouts back. "What are you talking about, my friend?"

Saebjorn stands up as soon as he has dialed the number and walks over to the bookshelf on the right of the bedroom window.

"We were playing some music just now that you said was chamber music," Havard shouts.

"Yes, Mahler. We were playing Mahler. Mahler's piano quartet," Armann says. Just as before, he sees no reason to shut the door while he urinates.

"That's what we were listening to," I hear Havard say to Jaime, "Mahler's piano quartet. Actual chamber music, the real thing. One hundred percent proof." Then he shouts: "Do you hear that, Armann? One hundred percent chamber music!"

Armann starts laughing and repeats Havard's last words. There is clearly some comradeship that connects them at this moment.

"You are a great chamber fan, aren't you Armann?" Havard carries on in the same loud voice.

Who else, apart from these two, would shout from one room to another about chamber music, I ask myself.

"Chamber fan?" Armann begins to pee into the toilet bowl, and considering the state he is in at the moment, I can't imagine that he will be more successful now than on the previous occasion. "You are fine fellows," he says in a low voice that can hardly be heard in the living room over the noise he is making.

"Hello?" Saebjorn has contacted one of my parents, who turns out to be my mother. "Yes, good evening. My name is Saebjorn, I'm a friend of Emil's. I am just checking to see if Emil is by any chance with you. He hasn't come? He hasn't called either? Yes, I'm at his place, there are two of us here, his friends. He was going to meet us here this evening after he arrived. What? Yes, there's also an old friend of his here, Havard. He spoke to you? Yes, he came here earlier today, as far as I know, and saw through the window that Emil was boiling water here so he . . . yes, no, he wasn't at home . . . so he climbed in through the window and took the water off the burner. That he forgot it? You mean that Emil should forget it? Yes, it is rather strange. He had unpacked his suitcases. It looked as if he had just nipped out."

Saebjorn listens to my mother for one or two minutes and nods in agreement with what she says. Something suddenly falls on to the floor, probably a book from the shelf, and Saebjorn carries on listening while he bends down to pick up the fallen object. "Yes, I think we will have to," he says finally, and I hear that the conversation is drawing to a close.

Armann flushes the toilet and goes back into the party without washing his hands. I'm about to try and make contact with Saebjorn before he leaves the room—I am even considering whispering to him—but he suddenly turns away from the bookshelf and rushes out. He is still talking to my mother. He tells her that there are two other people here, a young woman and a slightly older man who was with me on the plane. They are fine, just some people whom I seem to have invited home. Then he goes into the bathroom and asks my mother if I could have gone to visit Vigdis. It's not very probable but there must be some reason for me taking so long. It doesn't seem that he and my mother come to any conclusion. As soon as Saebjorn has said goodbye to her, he turns on the tap—probably to have a drink of water—and then goes back into the living room.

The piano quartet has started again, and as far as I can hear Armann is lecturing the other visitors on the music.

"Yes, wasn't it seventy-six?" I hear Saebjorn say. It sounds as though he had some doubt about the year and has now received confirmation that it was right.

"That must make all the difference," Havard says scornfully.

"Eighteen hundred seventy-six," Armann confirms.

I think of my son Halldor. Now he is lying in his bed in Amager, fast asleep in his Danish bed with his twin teddies by his head, completely ignorant of the fact that his father is lying awake under his own bed on Grettisgata and doesn't dare to come out because he has this dread of something that is impossible to explain.

Why don't you just go and say hello to your friends, daddy?

What are you doing there under the bed?

I'm just resting, Halldor. Just go back to sleep. No, I know it's not the most comfortable place. One mustn't always think of what is most comfortable.

"He was only sixteen," is yet another piece of information that Armann gives the others.

"And how old are you?" Havard asks. He's totally uninterested in Armann's precise age, but he's very eager to confirm his suspicion that once one reaches thirty everything starts going downhill.

They all seem the same age to me at this moment.

6

I feel as though almost a whole day has passed since I sat beside Armann in the plane. And yet it is only three or four hours since I came home, the same length of time it takes to play four CDs of average length. I'm getting a bit tired of the limited view I have, but by lifting the sheet about ten or twenty centimeters off the floor on my left I can see out of the bedroom window. The curtains are only half closed. Although the lampposts and the windows of the houses on the main street cast a little light, the darkness outside seems to be thick and viscous. I don't know why—perhaps hunger is bothering me—but when I look out into the darkness, I think of the black bean soup that I once ordered by mistake in a Brazilian restaurant in New York a few years ago. I was with Anna and her parents. They had invited us for a weekend trip two weeks after we had told them that we were expecting a child. That trip turned out to be an absolute disaster. Not because my in-laws were difficult in any way, I always got on well with them, but at that time Anna and I didn't have a penny to our name, and despite the fact that she was pregnant, or maybe exactly because she was, we didn't get on very well; we fought over every little detail. Just before we set out we had to hand over our Visa card into the demanding hands of the bank, and I felt awful—just like Anna did, not being able to buy herself clothes—flicking through the CDs in Tower Records without being able to buy even a couple of them. Or almost. I managed to hoard a few dollars and brought home one CD that I bought without telling Anna; it was a disc that I literally had to own and would never have forgiven myself for not bringing home, considering I had managed to find it in the first place. Today I brought home thirty-six discs, more than the years that I have lived. And probably more than the years I have left to live.

If time has some special role then I think it is two-fold: to take things away from one (if one can speak about Anna and Halldor having been taken away from me) and to give one something else instead (for instance the lottery prize I won)—something that doesn't replace the loss, but helps one to forget now and again what one has lost. Perhaps one can rely on time in these functions, but in all other aspects it is not possible. Suddenly a new age has dawned, the age in which one will disappear into one's grave. I've passed thirty, and as midnight is approaching on this day of my homecoming from abroad, I am lying under my bed and there are people in the living room biding their time until I appear. It seems as though time is going to disappoint them.

When I look out of the rather narrow bedroom window and see the lampposts that shine between the houses on Laugavegur, I remember a story that I read once about the first street lights in the city. Towards the end of the nineteenth century several lights were purchased—no doubt they were some sort of oil lamps—and the first one was set up on the lower slopes of Bankastraeti. I think it was in autumn or the beginning of winter, at least it had started to get dark in the evenings, and on the very day that the first street light was set up it was broken by someone who threw a stone at it. I can just imagine some Havard, some dirty lout in homespun pants, tramping down Laugavegur in the dark and not realizing what kind of light is down the hill on Bankastraeti. He walks faster towards it, and when he is standing in front of the lamppost, the first lamppost in the town of Reykjavik, he wonders why on earth someone is trying to light up the town; it's completely unnecessary to illuminate what goes on in the dark. He looks around, and in the dim light he sees a stone—just the right size to fit into his fist. He bends down, picks it up, gazes for a little while at the flame burning inside the lamp, and then steps back several paces, to avoid being under the broken glass when the stone shatters it.

The piano quartet has been removed and Elvis's voice comes out of the loudspeakers. Someone goes into the toilet and this time the door is closed. It sounds as though all the men are in the living room; Havard is talking (something about stereo equipment) and I hear Armann offer Jaime and Saebjorn a cigar, so it must be Greta who has gone to the toilet. I let the sheet fall to the floor and shut my eyes. I imagine her pulling down her black skirt—I try not to see the wet patch left by Armann on the floor beside the toilet—and then her panties; they are black too. Will she check to see if the seat is clean before she sits down? I try to hear what she is doing in the bathroom, but the music is so loud at the moment that I can't make out a thing. I suddenly feel as if these four men have become good friends, that they know each other well and have met to discuss something they have in common, something that only men talk about, something that Greta has inadvertently given them permission to talk about by disappearing into the toilet. After "Suspicious Minds" comes "Don't Cry Daddy," and that song adds to the relaxed atmosphere that seems to prevail in the living room. For a moment I long to take part, *to be on friendly terms with all the inmates of the place one lodges in*, but the next moment I am really glad that I am alone, all by myself.

There is a knock on the front door. I hear Greta flush the toilet and then another knock. Then there is a more insistent banging, like some sort of drumming practice. Saebjorn says he'll answer and I hear him walk towards the door. The drumming is still going on when he takes hold of the door knob.

7

"Does this place belong to Emil S. Halldorsson?" the person outside asks, and two or three men, whom I imagine are standing behind him, begin to laugh, like he said something really funny. It sounds like drunken laughter to me.

"Who are you?" Saebjorn asks, and I tell myself how ridiculous it is that I know who he is though I have never seen him.

"I'm looking for Vardi," he answers and the laughter, which it would be more correct to call giggling, carries on.

"There is no one called Vardi here."

"Are you sure?" the stranger says in disbelief. Then he shouts victoriously: "Who is this then!"

"Hi, Rikki," Havard says. He has obviously come out into the hall, but he clearly doesn't know quite how enthusiastically he should welcome his friend.

"If you didn't know," his friend says, "then you know now that he is Vardi. Havard Knutsson, criminal." All emphasis is placed on the last syllable of the word *criminal*.

I picture this Hinrik as a rather dubious character, but I am probably drawing an unnecessarily black image of him in my mind. One isn't necessarily bad just because one is an acquaintance of Havard; I was his acquaintance for a little while, and I imagine that some people have seen me in this light too. But I'm quite certain that it annoys Havard to be called a criminal in front of people who haven't the slightest idea that he actually is one.

The bathroom door opens. I turn my head quickly and lift up the sheet—far too abruptly I realize—but I'm too late to catch sight of Greta, she has gone into the hall.

"Aren't you going to invite us in?" Hinrik asks, and one of his mates adds in a rather childish whine, "Yes, how about it. Aren't you going to invite us in?"

"Who are they?" Saebjorn says and then Greta asks what is going on.

"It's alright, he's just a friend of mine." Havard explains, and I can imagine he is silently cursing Hinrik for dragging the whole band along too.

"What's up, Vardi?" Hinrik says, and I can just picture Saebjorn standing in the doorway blocking the entrance. "Aren't you going to let us in?"

"No one else is going to come in here," Saebjorn says decisively.

"They aren't stopping, it's alright," Havard says. "Just let me talk to them."

"What nonsense is this?" Hinrik says pitiably, and Havard asks him to be patient.

"If anyone has patience, I have, Vardi." My impression of him doesn't improve with hearing his voice.

Greta asks Havard to talk to her for a moment, and a few seconds later they appear in the bedroom. Hinrik asks Saebjorn if *he* is this fellow, Emil S. And while I listen to Havard and Greta, I can hear Hinrik explain to Saebjorn that Havard had called him earlier this evening and invited him to look in at the flat on Grettisgata.

"You're not to invite anyone else in," Greta says angrily to Havard, making sure that no one else can hear her. She tells him he has to understand that the flat is no dance hall, besides, I am not even at home and I'm the one who lives there, not them. Havard is quick to understand that she is right; he mumbles some kind of objection but then says he'll talk to Hinrik. He is just like that, this fellow. She can calm down. The front door is obviously still wide open, even I am getting rather cold, and I hear Greta shiver when she goes back out into the hall.

"What's going on?" Hinrik repeats. And Havard answers that there is nothing going on, he just can't let them in, something has come up. This friend of his doesn't seem quite ready to accept the fact that he can't come in.

"We have come all the way from Breidholt, Vardi," he says accusingly. "There are forty degrees of frost outside, and we are freezing to death here."

I can imagine how they are dressed, and I'm not surprised that they want to come in.

"You are going to play somewhere, aren't you?" Havard says. "I'll look in afterwards."

"I haven't seen you for several years and I'm not even allowed in. What kind of pussy lives here anyway?"

"I'll see you later, Rikki. Sorry. I'll come along later."

"OK?" Saebjorn says, clearly getting ready to shut the door.

"Nothing is OK," Hinrik complains, and Saebjorn shuts the door in the middle of Hinrik saying that they didn't come all the way here, to Grettisgata, just to be sent away. The drumming on the door begins again, and despite the fact that the door is locked and the music is on, I can hear angry voices outside; a whole band making a scene late at night in the freezing cold in the middle of a residential area. One of them shouts out swear words in English and another sings something that sounds like a football supporter song. That's wonderful, I think to myself. Before they finally go off, they drum something on the kitchen or living room window, and for a moment I wish that they would break the window, so Saebjorn would take action and send Havard off with those troublemaking friends of his. Though he has said he is going to meet them afterwards, I have no real hope that it will be soon.

"Who were those gentlemen?" Armann asks, unable to conceal the fact that he is rather drunk.

"An old friend of mine," Havard says, as if he doesn't want to discuss it further.

"An extremely polite fellow," Saebjorn says sarcastically.

Only two or three minutes have passed since Hinrik and his friends left when there is another knock on the door. That must be me, I say to myself; I can't think of anyone else who could be on the way here.

"Here he comes!" Armann calls out, and I'm sure that all the others here are expecting it to be me. "Our friend on Grettisgata!"

As the front door is opened, the music is turned down and a glass, or something fragile, falls on the floor but doesn't break.

"Armann!" Greta shouts.

"Good evening," Havard says, and I hear Greta tell Armann that he can't just empty the ashtray on the floor, it's bad enough that he has dirtied the whole table.

"Yes, that's possible, I came here at lunchtime," Havard agrees with the person standing outside. "No, it is alright. They were just some guys, they won't come back."

I can't hear who he is talking to, only the frail voice of an elderly man, but there is no doubt that it is my neighbor Tomas. He must have heard the noise Hinrik and his friends made and has come to see that everything is alright.

"Yes, you spoke to him today, didn't you?" Havard continues. "Yes. No we are just waiting for him, he nipped out. You live next door, yes? I'll tell him. Alright."

Then he shuts the door.

"It's good to have neighbors who keep an eye on you," Havard says cheerfully when he comes back into the living room. "At least one isn't all alone in the world."

"Who was that?" Saebjorn asks.

"Some fellow in an anorak, one of Emil's neighbors."

"Good," Armann says, and it seems that he is falling asleep, his voice sounds so tired. "That's good."

"Yes, don't you think you would make a good neighbor for Emil?" Havard asks, and I hear a cork being removed from a bottle; it is either cognac or Greta's red wine.

"Not in the state you are in," Greta says with a laugh. "Armann, my friend, won't you lie down? I think you are rather tired."

Armann mumbles something weakly, Greta's assumption is obviously correct, then he barks suddenly, and quite clearly, considering the state he is in:

"*Let this be our final will at the great noontide.*"

"Wait a minute?" Havard exclaims. "What was that? Our final will, what?"

"Our final will at the great noontide," Armann repeats. Now his voice is more in keeping with his condition.

"But Armann, aren't you just a little late with it? It's nearly midnight. The time is ten, nearly eleven at night."

"Noontide . . . midnight." He drawls as if these big words were full of lead. "Who was that outside? Who is . . ." He seems to be completely collapsing.

"Relax, Armann," Greta says encouragingly.

Jaime suggests that they help him into the bed, but Greta would rather he rested on the sofa. I can tell Saebjorn is disgusted that such an elderly man has drunk himself stupid, and I tell myself that my friend's rationalism can sometimes be utterly unbearable.

"He didn't need much," is the only comment that Havard has to make about Armann.

"Noontide . . . noon can't come round unless there is midnight first." Armann carries on.

Another antithesis from the mouth of the linguist. Noon, the warmest time of day, the opposite of midnight, the coldest time, when people search for warmth, when they want homes, alcohol, duvets, embraces, to enter one another.

"Evening comes for each one of us," he carries on with equal difficulty. "Our last will . . . we have high hopes at noon . . . but all hope has died by midnight."

"That is really profound, Armann!" Havard is amazed at what seems to be Armann's grand finale.

"The glasses . . ." he asks. Greta answers by saying "there, there," and tells him to lay his head down, everything is alright, he should just rest.

"Have my glasses been found?" he repeats in a weak voice. Havard reminds him that he came here to fetch them; they are lying on the table.

"Please help yourselves," Armann groans. He sounds as if he is talking in his sleep. "Help yourselves, my good friends."

8

I think of what Armann said to me on the plane: that he often felt he was in some kind of limbo. Reflecting on it, I feel it is strange that he should talk about limbo being his favorite word; that word has always made me feel rather uncomfortable. Apart from its cheerful sound, which is reminiscent of words such as bimbo and mambo or something of the sort, its meaning isn't exactly positive, and the first image that arises in my mind is of little children playing some innocent game. Then I hear heavy music and all at once the children are inside some dark limbo, from which they never escape. Armann is too old to take part in this strange game, but when I picture him on the sofa, I think it is probable that he is in some other kind of limbo, perhaps the one he tried to explain to me on the plane without me understanding what he meant.

When Greta asks if I have a dustpan and brush, Saebjorn answers that she is bound to find something like that in the big cupboard in the kitchen. She goes into the kitchen, opens the cupboard, and walks back into the living room, whistling a tune I recognize.

"Wasn't that somebody knocking?"

I hadn't heard anything.

"No doubt this neighbor again," Havard suggests.

"I'm quite sure someone was knocking," Greta says again, but she doesn't seem willing to go to the door. Besides, it should be the job of one of the men. I hear someone stand up and the front door opens, but nothing happens to show that Greta was right.

"Have a look outside," Saebjorn calls out from the living room, and then I hear someone dial a number on his cell phone.

"I don't see anyone," Jaime answers. But it sounds like he is going outside as Saebjorn suggested; the door is still open and I can feel the cold come in, as if it's crawling along the floor and creeping into every corner of the flat.

Saebjorn has started to talk to someone on the phone. He says he is at my place. He and Jaime had come here to fetch some CDs I had bought for them, but he'll be there quite soon. I imagine he is talking to his girlfriend, Klara.

I feel sorry for Jaime when he comes back in and closes the front door. He is shivering and tells them through his chattering teeth that he didn't see anyone outside. Saebjorn switches off his phone and suggests to Jaime that they get going.

"It's something supernatural," Havard says. "Isn't it just Emil's ghost? Hasn't he just had an accident and . . ."

"Don't say that!" Greta stops him.

"Well, things happen," Havard answers indifferently.

"Isn't it just Emil in person?" Saebjorn suggests, more cheerful than he has been up until now.

"I must have imagined it," Greta says, and I think I have to agree with her. At least it wasn't me.

While she is tidying up in the living room—it sounds as though she is moving things and carrying glasses into the kitchen—Saebjorn says that maybe I didn't feel like having any visitors this evening and had made myself scarce before they arrived. I know he is joking, but I begin to wonder if Havard, who hasn't yet made any comment on Saebjorn's idea, is pondering whether there is some truth in it.

"Not to mention the fact that you climbed through the window so Emil hasn't been able to come home again," Saebjorn continues, still with the same humor.

Havard doesn't respond.

"Maybe he is trying to frighten us by knocking on the door," Jaime suggests. "He wants us to think it is a ghost."

For a moment I feel as if I'm taking part in an adventure story for teenagers, that I, the missing man whom everyone is searching for, can't be bothered being in the story any longer and have started reading it instead, without telling the other characters that I have been found and that they can stop searching. But I'm beginning to worry that this conversation will lead to some conclusion. Havard, who doesn't normally keep his thoughts to himself, hasn't commented on my friends' speculations, and I am really afraid that he will stand up any moment now and look for me in the only suitable hiding place in the flat.

"Is he completely out?" Saebjorn asks. He is most likely referring to Armann. He hasn't made a sound since he told all the others to help themselves.

"He has gone completely," Greta answers, and I think of limbo again; he has gone off to his own private mysterious realm. "Oh, he's really sweet like that," she adds.

I was waiting for Havard to stand up and follow his suspicion into the bedroom, but it hasn't happened yet. On the other hand, Saebjorn asks Greta to talk to him and the next moment they are standing in the hall between the bathroom and the bedroom.

"What is the time?" I hear Havard ask Jaime, but can't concentrate on what is happening in the living room because Saebjorn has started talking to Greta.

"Are you going to stay here longer?" he asks in a whisper, and she nods in reply. She is going to wait a while for me.

"Do you think you can keep an eye on them? It doesn't look like this Havard is going to leave straightaway."

"Keep an eye on them?" Greta asks, no doubt with a smile.

"I have to go, perhaps I'll come back later or at least phone."

Greta laughs in reply and says she is used to looking after such little boys. Besides, Armann isn't likely to get into trouble at the moment. Saebjorn shushes her and asks her to keep her voice down. They move into my bedroom.

"I just don't trust this fellow Havard completely," Saebjorn continues in a whisper.

Really? I say to my friend, though more to myself here on this side of the blue sheet.

"I mean, there are things of value in here," he adds, almost as if he is letting her in on a secret. I know exactly what he considers valuable. He is thinking about the CDs, the thirty-six discs I have just bought, and the other two-thousand in the specially made shelves, as well as all the records—my collection which, to my surprise, none of these guests who have come here today for the first time seem to have admired. Saebjorn, on the other hand, hasn't caught sight of the valuables which Havard brought—the ship and the one hundred and fifty year old book which are lying here in front of my feet.

"You don't have to worry about Havard," Greta says. "I think he is about to go, wasn't he going to meet his friend downtown?"

It's obvious that Greta thinks Saebjorn is worrying unnecessarily. She laughs and whispers that it's not a problem. She'll wait here and Havard will go soon, it's not as though there is a criminal in the place. They go back out again and Havard meets them with a question, do they know the name of the fiancée of the former president of Argentina? Miss Universe from Chile. He says he can't understand that Jaime doesn't know it, he comes from Chile and doesn't know the name of the former Miss Universe who also came from Chile. If I know Jaime well it's something that he absolutely does not want to know.

"Cecilia Bolocco!" Greta says without thinking.

"Hey, you're right!" Havard shouts. "Now I remember: Cecilia Bolocco! Greta! You know it! And the man from Chile hasn't a clue what I am talking about!"

"Who do you think tries to remember such things, Havard?" When Greta says that, when she tries to defend Jaime, who I'm sure has become nervous around Havard, I am quite certain that we have a lot in common, that our short acquaintance in the bus has convinced us both that we have some kind of connection.

While Havard continues to fuss over Jaime's ignorance, Saebjorn asks his friend if he wants a ride in the car, he is going to look in at Klara's and then go home, he has to wake up early the next morning. I imagine that Jaime is on his way to work—he works as a night watchman for the broadcasting company—and it turns out that I am right. When he accepts the ride, he says he has to return home before he goes to work. I know they don't need to be reminded to take the CDs with them, but I wish I could ask Saebjorn to take Havard with him. Or at least offer him a ride.

"So you are leaving?" Havard says, and it doesn't sound as if he regrets their departure.

Saebjorn asks if he wants to come with them, he can drive him downtown, but Havard declines the offer. He says he is going to wait a little longer for me, he isn't going downtown before eleven-thirty at the earliest. "Thanks very much just the same," he says in an exaggerated manner, which I know must annoy Saebjorn.

While my friends are leaving I use the opportunity to turn over. It is a great relief to lie on my back, and I stretch my stiff legs too. I hear Greta say goodbye to Saebjorn and Jaime, and they seem to leave without saying a word to Havard. I gaze up at the mattress, up at the drooping, starless night sky, this worn material that has been the basis for my sleep for far too long. And for the first time since I crawled under the bed there is complete silence in the flat. Nothing is said for perhaps thirty seconds, there is no music, I can only hear my own breathing. And it is uncomfortable. It is as though Greta has frozen still; she seems to have accompanied Saebjorn and Jaime to the front door, but I don't hear her come back. I feel almost as if I am hiding from no one, and, strange as it may sound, I am relieved when Havard says "well, well" and announces that he is going to have one more drink. I'm waiting for him to say that he is going when he has finished his drink, but Greta takes over: "How did you and Emil get to know each other?" she asks.

9

I expect Havard to answer Greta's question with some nonsense, some rubbish about our long friendship, but I'm relieved when he says that we don't really know each other much:

"We really don't know each other at all," he says, and Greta sounds amazed. She says something I can't make out because some kind of banging drowns out her words; someone seems to be hitting the back or seat of an armchair. Then Havard says that he was with me in England several years ago, we had been working together and some relative of mine had sent us to London to look after his animals.

"Yes, you told us earlier, didn't you?" Greta interrupts. "What kind of animals were they?" Her voice is full of childish enthusiasm, which, I have to say, surprises me.

"He had a rabbit and some kind of guinea pig," Havard answers. "A snowy white albino guinea pig. Then there was the lizard. An iguana lizard. Some kind of miniature prehistoric monster. And a cat."

Greta gets excited at this information. She laughs and says it's like a whole zoo and tells him that she has been looking after some little hamsters for the past two weeks. "Well, sort of," she adds: she has been staying with her sister in London too. There were two little hamsters in the bedroom where she slept, really crazy little things which slept all day and kept her awake all night. Then one of them gave birth to several babies, which it had been trying to eat when they found him. "Or her, I should say."

"That's exactly what these stupid creatures do," Havard says.

"How do you mean?"

"They eat their offspring."

"Yes, but only if they think someone is going to take them away," Greta answers, as if objecting to Havard's low opinion of hamsters. "They don't have babies just to eat them," she adds.

"People should not have such animals in their homes," Havard says. "It always ends in some sort of trouble. But, on the other hand it's alright to have a dog. One can even make money on dogs." He tells her that we had a daily wage in London, that my relative had paid us a small daily allowance for looking after his house and animals, but she could just imagine how far that went to keep us. So he had started betting on dog races and that had helped us to a certain extent. There's money to be made on dogs if you know how to play.

"But did you know that Emil was coming today?" Greta asks. I can imagine that she wants to change the subject, that she doesn't believe a word of the nonsense Havard is telling her. "I mean, was Emil expecting you?"

"I'm sure he was. Isn't he just on the way to visit his girlfriend. This Vigdis? He had at least started to write her an email, I saw it on the computer in there just now. Maybe he stopped somewhere on the way, no doubt some bar. Even I stopped at several bars on the way here today."

"But the water? Wasn't there water boiling on the stove when you came here?"

"He just forgot it. I mean, people forget. He probably forgot that I was going to visit him too."

It is difficult to say what Greta thinks about this friend of mine who says in one breath that we don't know each other at all and then in the next that I was expecting him to come for a visit. And what does she think about me—some fellow who really wants a date but obviously has a girlfriend, doesn't turn up for the date, and lets four other men come in his place?

"But you haven't met for some time?" Greta asks.

"No," Havard answers curtly, and when he starts talking again he raises his voice, as if he is talking to Greta from another room. "I have been living in Sweden. We haven't seen each other for five years. I really only came today to return something I borrowed from his relative there in London."

"What, something you borrowed five years ago!" Greta doesn't try to hide her amazement.

"Yes," he answers. "An old book and some kind of carved model of a ship. It's in there beside his bed."

In there beside his bed? I suddenly feel very uncomfortable; I grow hot all over, without any sweat appearing, and some sort of irritation spreads through my body. In there beside his bed? In there beside *me*?

"And what are you doing in *Sweden*?" Greta asks. "Not looking after some animals again?"

Havard laughs and is about to say something when Greta interrupts him; she has to phone home. She seems to go into the kitchen, the sound of her dialing comes from there. She has to wait a little while before there is an answer, then she says hello to her mother and asks if her daughter is asleep. It sounds as though her mother has managed to get the little girl to sleep. She begins to talk about something that Greta isn't very interested in—something to do with the family, some problem that I can't imagine Greta wants to get involved in, as she is just back from abroad and full of thoughts of me perhaps. Or Havard; how she can get rid of him. I am listening hard to hear Greta's reply when Havard suddenly comes into the bedroom and stops in the middle of the room. I feel one hundred percent sure that he will address me or, without saying a word, just drag me out from under the bed like some criminal on the run. But instead he sits down in the chair in front of the computer and starts to unlace his shoes. Of course I am in no position to peep out from under the sheet, but it is clear that his shoes are rather tight; he has to pull hard to get them off.

Greta is still talking to her mother. Havard stands up from the chair; if I'm not mistaken, he is undoing his pants. Something hard bangs into the arm of the chair or desk—probably the buckle on his belt. I hear his pants slide down to the floor, and then Havard sits down on the edge of the bed. He makes some kind of drumming sound with his mouth, a sound that forms a melody. I try to anticipate where the springs will press down into my body if he lies down on the bed. My speculations are accurate, the mattress sags down about ten centimeters when Havard lies down, and the springs poke into the lower part of my stomach and my groin. It doesn't cause any great pain, but I swear to myself; why the hell does the man have to let me know physically that he has found out where I am? He sighs with pleasure, and I can feel him stretching. Greta is clearly trying to finish off her telephone conversation; I heard her say earlier that she would probably be a little late coming home and now she repeats it to her mother.

"Come and talk to me, Greta! I'm here in the bedroom!" Havard calls out as soon as she is off the phone. I hear her come into the hall and then suddenly there is a knock at the door. Greta asks him to wait. I'm not particularly surprised that, despite the fact Havard is lying on the bed, he doesn't seem to be at all worried that I might be the person on the doorstep. The front door is opened and Greta calls out "Hello?" into the dark. Havard is amused; he laughs, as if he is saying to himself that of course there was no one outside. Greta must be hearing things. She calls out my name and now I'm afraid that she will wake up or disturb Bella in the flat above or give Tomas a reason to knock again. I don't expect Armann to be woken up by the sound of her voice. She calls again in a loud whisper, "Hello? Emil?" almost as if she expects me to be hiding out there in the cold and doesn't want anyone else to notice me. I wish I could answer her; I long to be able to answer her.

But I wasn't the one who knocked on the door.

10

I wasn't the one who knocked, I repeat to myself. Of all those who have come here today I am the only one who hasn't knocked on the door. I opened the door with a key. I let myself in. It's as though I have to remind myself that it is *I* who live here.

When Greta has closed the door she calls to Havard: "Didn't you say that the man who knocked earlier was wearing an anorak?"

"Yes, was it him?" Havard answers, and I can just see the grin on his face as he lies there half naked just above me.

"No, I didn't see anyone," Greta says, sounding surprised. "I don't know who it could have been."

She seems to be in the living room.

"I was wearing an anorak," Havard calls out cheerfully. "Maybe it was me? Maybe I was coming a second time? Can you be bothered to come in here?"

She tells him to wait. I imagine she is having a drink. Then I hear her using her lighter, and I recall the moment when we stood outside the airport smoking together. I haven't had a cigarette for four or five hours. Then she opens the front door again, as if she is trying to convince herself that there is no one outside.

"The second coming of Howard Knutsson," Havard whispers to himself and lifts up his body so that his weight moves from his behind to his legs. With this distribution of weight the springs press down near my face; they are only one or two centimeters away from my nose. Then I hear him drop something onto the floor. I lift the sheet a fraction and see his underwear lying there; they are white, and I notice that they are the same brand I wear. His pants, on the other hand, have been put on the chair. I imagine he is still wearing his shirt.

Suddenly it feels as if the sheet is pulled—it goes up several centimeters. Havard tosses about on the bed, and he seems to be spreading the duvet over his body.

"I want to show you something!" he calls out.

He is going to show her something! A little something! He is probably under the duvet; he is relaxed now, so the springs are down over my stomach again. I hear Greta enter the room.

"I thought you were going." Greta sounds startled to see him in bed.

"Come and sit down," Havard says and tells her to take the pants off the chair. "I'm going in a minute, I was just so cold in there."

Since the sheet has been lifted up from the floor I can see Greta walk to the chair. She picks up the pants and puts them on top of Halldor's toy box. As she sits down I wriggle as far as I can towards the wall, so that she is less likely to notice me.

"How do you like this suit that I bought today?" Havard asks.

"This one? Did you buy it today?"

"I bought it on Laugavegur. Just before I came here. The jacket is in the living room."

Hasn't she noticed his underwear on the floor? Isn't she going to say anything about him being in bed?

"See here," he says. I feel him roll over in the bed, and he seems to be getting something from the floor. "This is what I was going to give back to him. I came all the way from Sweden to return it," he adds proudly.

Greta stretches towards the bed. The chair creaks; I imagine that she takes the book and the ship.

"Moby . . . Dick," Havard says with a laugh and then asks: "Were you calling home because of your daughter?"

Greta says yes; her daughter has to go to school the next morning and didn't fall asleep straight away when her grandmother was looking after her. She was rather excited because her mother had just come home.

"I know all about it," Havard says.

"Yes, of course, you have a daughter too. How old did you say she was?"

"My daughter? How old do *you* think she is?"

"I would guess about nine or ten, from seeing the photo."

"She is ten," Havard answers.

"But, wait a moment, didn't you say just now that she was eight?"

"She *was* eight. Now she is ten."

"Was she never nine then?"

"She's no normal child," Havard answers with a laugh. "You noticed that she was holding the Bible, didn't you? Completely of her own free will."

"But where can I have seen you before?" Greta asks. "I'm quite sure I have seen you somewhere before. You don't have a brother who looks like you, do you?"

"Well, I am a twin," Havard says. "The other Havard lives here in Reykjavik."

"Where in Reykjavik?"

"Somewhere in the eastern part of town. Somewhere near Hlemmur, I think."

"You think?" Greta asks with a laugh.

"I haven't a clue where he lives," Havard answers with typical carelessness.

"What, do you mean to say that you don't know where your brother lives?"

"Hey, am I supposed to look after my brother?" he says and repeats that he lives somewhere in East Reykjavik.

"Why didn't you tell me you had a brother?" Greta asks and is no doubt referring to the time, just after she arrived, when she said that she thought she recognized him. "Then I must have seen your brother in town, I was so sure I had seen you before."

"You mean that you remember my face from having seen my brother somewhere in town?"

"It must be that," Greta answers. "What does your brother do?"

"He's in some dodgy business. I have no idea what he does, I haven't heard from him for a long time."

"What's he called?"

"Havard."

"No really, what's he called?" Greta repeats in disbelief.

"Havard."

"You aren't both called Havard?"

"No."

"What are you called then?"

"Gisli."

"Come on."

"Gisli Norstedt," Havard answers.

"And your brother is called Havard?"

"Havard Norstedt."

"Are you identical twins?"

Havard laughs rather nastily at Greta's question.

"You must really be, seeing you are so alike."

"Yes, we broke out of the same shell. We both came from the same rotten egg."

Greta laughs, and Havard asks if Armann is still in the living room.

"Of course Armann is still there," she says. "Hey, I'm going to fetch my glass."

She is going to fetch her glass, I tell myself, and Havard asks if there is enough red wine left for a second glass. She says she thinks so, stands up from the chair, and goes out.

"Don't be long, I'm so terribly frightened of the dark," he shouts after her.

I hear her open a zip in the living room and then she seems to be rummaging about; I imagine her with her hand in her bag looking for something. I don't dare to imagine what she needs from her bag. Havard moves about in the bed. I notice his underwear on the floor and recall one morning at Brooke Road.

It was our third or fourth day in England. I woke up about nine o'clock. The sun was shining and, as I couldn't get back to sleep, I went down into the kitchen to fetch some Alka-Seltzer. We had been drinking whisky and beer late into the night, and I hadn't gone to sleep until six. Havard was still wide awake at the time, and he was playing music from Orn's or Osk's collection. When I entered the kitchen in the morning, newly wakened, I saw him standing out in the garden in his underwear—I was sure he hadn't gone to sleep—and he was holding Moby, the albino guinea pig. There were two empty beer cans beside the sink. He didn't see me there beside the window; he had his back towards me, and he lifted the guinea pig up like he was holding a trophy. Then he cuddled the animal and seemed to be stroking it. I remember the music coming from the living room; it was something similar to what he had been playing when I went to sleep earlier that morning. He seemed to be about to put the guinea pig down, and when he turned round suddenly I ducked back behind the wall by the window. But when I looked out again I saw that he hadn't put the animal down yet. Now he was holding it at arm's length and was talking to it. Then he cuddled it up to his naked chest. When he put it gently down on the pavement, I grabbed hold of the Alka-Seltzer box and rushed back upstairs to the bathroom to get a glass of water.

I didn't see Havard again until about two o'clock that day, soon after I had woken up. He was lying asleep on the sofa in the living room, still just wearing his underwear, with the sun streaming in. On the table in front of him there was a squashed Holsten beer can, and in a large ashtray lay the crumpled wrappings from the second cigarette carton he had bought in the duty-free store at home. I remember I couldn't bear to look at him lying there in the bright sunshine, with his weak mouth hanging open and one of his hands dangling down to the floor, and I think it was Elvis that I put in the CD player at full volume in order to wake him up. But he carried on sleeping, and he barely made a sound when I took hold of his shoulder and shook him. I couldn't bear to stay in the same house as that smelly lump, so I went out to the book bar for a little while, then took the seventy three bus to town and went into the cinema in Leicester Square.

It wasn't until I got home, at around nine o'clock in the evening, that Havard woke up. He jumped up like a dog when he heard the door slam, met me in the kitchen where he fetched a can of beer from the fridge, went back to the sofa, lay down, and put Elvis on again.

However, here on Grettisgata at the moment, there is gentle piano music playing in the living room. I don't recognize it right away; I imagine it is something that Greta brought with her, but then I hear it is Alicia de Larrocha playing music by Enrique Granados. Greta pours red wine into the glasses and mutters something quietly to herself, which probably means she has spilled some wine. Havard begins to whistle "Habanera" and stops suddenly when Greta comes back into the room.

She is barefoot. I had tried to pull the sheet very gently, hoping to hide myself better, but considering how much I see of Greta as she tiptoes carefully towards the stool by the desk—she is no doubt trying not to spill anything from the glasses—the sheet seems to be just as high above the floor as before. When she has only one or two steps left to reach the chair, she accidentally puts her right foot in Havard's underwear. She stops and gives a little kick to try and shake them off her toes, but they seem to be glued to her. She bends down and places the glasses on the table, probably beside the keyboard.

"What?" Havard asks with a laugh.

"Nothing," Greta answers and uses her left foot to loosen the underwear from the right one.

Bragi Ólafsson is the author of several books of poetry and short stories, and four novels, including *Time Off*, which was nominated for the Icelandic Literature Prize in 1999 (as was *The Pets*), and *Party Games*, for which Bragi received the DV Cultural Prize in 2004. His most recent novel—*The Ambassador*—was a finalist for the 2008 Nordic Literature Prize and received the Icelandic Bookseller's Award as best novel of the year. Bragi is one of the founders of the publishing company Smekkleysa (Bad Taste), and has translated Paul Auster's *The Glass City* into Icelandic. He is also a former bass player with The Sugarcubes, the internationally successful pop group that featured Björk as the lead vocalist.

J anice Balfour was born in Scotland and relocated to Iceland in 1972, where she studied literature and Italian at the University of Iceland. She began translating articles and texts for museums shortly thereafter. In addition to Bragi Olafsson, she has translated two collections of short stories by Gyrðir Elíasson (currently unpublished in English).

O pen Letter—the University of Rochester's nonprofit, literary translation press—is one of only a handful of publishing houses dedicated to increasing access to world literature for English readers. Publishing twelve titles in translation each year, Open Letter searches for works that are extraordinary and influential, works that we hope will become the classics of tomorrow.

Making world literature available in English is crucial to opening our cultural borders, and its availability plays a vital role in maintaining a healthy and vibrant book culture. Open Letter strives to cultivate an audience for these works by helping readers discover imaginative, stunning works of fiction and by creating a constellation of international writing that is engaging, stimulating, and enduring.

Current and forthcoming titles from Open Letter include works from France, Norway, Brazil, Lithuania, Iceland, and numerous other countries.

www.openletterbooks.org